THE 100 KILO CLUB

Simon Gandolfi

The
100 KILO
CLUB

Wildwood House London

First published 1975
© 1975 by Simon Gandolfi

Wildwood House Ltd, 1 Wardour Street, London W1V 3HE

ISBN 0 7045 0162 7

Printed in Great Britain by Biddles of Guildford

For Ubi in the hope that she is still alive; for Jean Jacques sweating out one more monsoon; for Yenner and Hassan; for Philippe, Elisbette and that magnificent Swiss; and for Vanessa, Walking John, Hamish and Jeannie; for Blind George last heard of riding a Rolls convertible close to Laguna Beach and for Jesse and Ley now out in the islands – names, so many names ... but to you all with love and with gratitude for a great trip.

BOOK ONE

In the dime stores and bus stations
People talk of situations
Read books repeat quotations
Draw conclusions on the wall.
Some speak of the future
My love, she speaks softly.
She knows there's no success like failure
And that failure's no success at all.

Bob Dylan

0935 HOURS. MONDAY. SEPTEMBER 17th, 1973.
STOCKHOLM. HAMNGATAN 18-20 EPA' DEPART-
MENT STORE.

Outside it was raining – not umbrella hard, but sufficiently to
make appear natural the headscarf she wore and the turned-up
collar of her raincoat. Threading her way quickly through the
crowd of early shoppers, she reached the elevators. She got out
on the fourth floor, then crossed directly to the bank of
telephone booths. She chose the centre box, glanced at her
watch, checked the number on the slip of paper she had tucked
in the cuff of her glove, fed øre into the slot, dialled and waited.

'Arlanda Airport,' came the voice of a young telephonist.
'S.A.S. Information.'

'Extension 41, please.'

'Putting you through . . . ' And then a man's voice, 'S.A.S.
Traffic Manager, good morning, can I help you?'

'Good morning. Your flight 401 to Copenhagen and New
York – there is a bomb on this flight.'

0945 HOURS. MONDAY. SEPTEMBER 17th, 1973.
COPENHAGEN. PRISON.

The warden glanced down at the paper in his hand then looked
up the long narrow stairwell. Steep iron stairs led to iron
gangways, wire netting between the gangways to catch
would-be suicides, four long tiers of cells.

'415,' he shouted.

'415,' the turnkey called back.

The American heard. Stubbing out his cigarette, he picked up his overnight bag. The key turned in the lock. Quick goodbye to the guard. Down the stairs with his own shoes feeling dangerously light after nineteen months in wooden clogs. First gate. Second gate. Reception office and two plain-clothes policemen waiting for him by the desk.

'Sign here ... here ... here,' This from the duty clerk. Brief pause. 'Good luck.'

The American smiled. 'Thanks,' he said.

'Let's go,' ordered the taller of the two policemen.

More keys, the last gate, then the door and the courtyard. A white Volvo stood backed up close to the door. The car was a four-seater two-door model. The driver sat waiting behind the wheel.

'In the back.'

'Don't I get to put my bag in the trunk?' the American protested. He gestured at his clean grey trousers and navy blazer. 'Or do I have to get all mussed up?'

The tall policeman had the car door open. The American turned to the other one who shrugged and smiled. 'Help yourself,' he said. He pushed up the lid of the trunk. *Clang* as he closed it. Metal on metal. Gaol sound.

Christ! the American thought, was that memory going to be with him the rest of his life? Then he was in the back of the Volvo – the seat behind the driver, the young policeman in beside him and then the tall one up front. More signatures at the main gates. Gates open. Through.

'Am I allowed to smoke?' the American asked.

The young policeman smiled. 'You're free,' he said.

'Till I get to the States.'

'How long will your sentence be?'

The American shrugged, lit his cigarette and blew smoke forward at the open window. 'Maximum five and ten,' he said.

'Fifteen years.' The policeman whistled. 'Jesus!'

The American blew more smoke and shrugged again. 'I won't get max,' he said. 'No way – and there's a chance for parole after one third.' Then he was concentrating on the sidewalk. Chicks! Tits. Asses. Legs. Chicks, chicks and more chicks.

'Look good?' the young policeman asked.

'Good enough to eat,' the American cracked and they both laughed.

'We'll have time for a beer at the airport,' the policeman promised him.

So it would be the young one, the American thought. Good. 'Who's buying?' he asked.

'Me, the first,' the policeman told him. 'Danish hospitality.'

The American laughed again. 'Nineteen months *and* a beer!' Then they were at the airport. A quick wave from the driver as they stood on the sidewalk, bag out of the trunk, then across the lobby to the S.A.S. desk with the two policemen walking right up close to him.

'Check your baggage or will you take it with you, Sir?'

'I'll carry it,' he told the girl. She nodded, gave him a smile which left him shy for a moment, then handed his ticket and boarding card to the young policeman.

'Let's go.' This from the tall escort. Friendly!

Still as a tight threesome, they turned left and up the steps to emigration. The young policeman slid the American Embassy repatriation order through the window together with the boarding card.

Stamp. Stamp. 'Have a good trip.' Danish courtesy, not sarcasm, and the American smiled.

'Thanks,' he said. Then they were through the gate and walking across the departure lounge to the bar – two of them. The tall policeman had gone without even a goodbye.

'His wife left him,' the young one explained. 'He got home two nights back and she'd gone. Left him a note propped on the kitchen table.'

'He deserve it?'

'Pretty much – you want that beer?'

Ice-cold Carlsberg and the Tannoy announcement. 'Scandinavian Airways regret to announce their flight 401 to New York will be delayed one hour.'

'Now what?' the American asked.

The policeman shrugged. 'Come on – let's find out.'

They carried their full glasses over towards the inquiry desk. A crowd had already gathered. 'Hey, Miss,' the policeman called to a reserve hostess hurrying to help out at the counter. He had his police identity card in his hand. 'What's happening?'

'Bomb hoax in Stockholm,' she told him. 'Fourth in ten days. They had to search the aircraft.'

'Jesus!' the American swore. 'That's all I need.'

'Scared of flying?' the policeman asked as they found a free bench and sat down.

'Some,' the American admitted.

'How about that to cheer you up?'

With her back to them, a hostess stood bending to fuss over an elderly lady in a wheel-chair. The hostess was plump and her skirt was tight – tight enough to split. The American gave a low whistle and looked away. Over at the transit desk a tall Black in his late twenties stood chatting up the counter girl. Dark-blue suit, white shirt, dark tie, he looked like a token spade from the State Department. He carried a crocodile-skin brief-case in his right hand and held a bunch of tickets and boarding passes in the other. The American watched the Black for a moment, then glanced down at his watch – 10:28. 'Want another beer?' he asked.

'You're paying,' the policeman told him. Digging an envelope out of his inside jacket pocket, he slit it and handed the American two ten-kroner bills then watched him walk over to the bar, collect the beers and bring them back.

'This is the last call for flight 213 to Geneva,' called the Tannoy. 'Exit 8.'

The American put the glasses on the table. 'Mind if I get a paper?' he asked.

'Do you have enough money?'

The American checked his change. 'Just on,' he said. 'Watch my bag?'

The policeman nodded and the American strolled over to the

paper kiosk. The magazine section was at the back. So was the Black.

'Would Mister George Katz, passenger to Geneva, please proceed immediately to Exit 8,' called the Tannoy. 'Mister George Katz, passenger to Geneva, Exit 8.'

The American bent down to look at a copy of *Playboy* on the bottom shelf. Then he stood up. He had a ticket, boarding pass and passport in his left hand and a crocodile-skin brief-case in his right.

'Move baby!' the Black whispered. 'Ten days to full moon.'

'Who's hanging around?' the American whispered back. Then he was through the rear entrance of the kiosk and walking fast down the long corridor to Exit 8.

CHAPTER ONE

'Ten days to full moon,' Black Jack had whispered to Pleasure at Copenhagen Airport.

After nineteen months of moon through the bars, now it was a free moon – Ibiza full moon in mid-September with the herb scent of the dry Mediterranean hills baked into the night so thick Pleasure had to shout aloud to release his joy as he rode his red-tanked Bultaco Matador straight on up at the floating goal of a spaced-out acid party with no one freaking and the stars as clear and steady as punctuation marks.

He parked his bike at the start of the last rocky rise up to Dutch Ned's *finca*. There were no other houses for a mile around. He'd already smoked three pipes and was moving so lightly he had to hold on to the bushes, just to keep himself down. The drums met him. Filled him. The red light of a bonfire danced down through the candelabra pines. He danced too – a sort of soft-shoe shuffle up the mountainside.

The white washed walls of the *finca* were dyed soft rose by the fire – a rose movie screen on which were projected the swaying shadows of a hundred heads. Rhythm beat: sticks tapping sticks, hands clapping, drums, stone on stone, and everyone too gone out of their minds for speech – no need for it. Egos surrendered to the whole, all they could individually do was gasp – gasp their bewilderment at so much ecstasy – or occasionally get it sufficiently together to roll a joint. This last was a career not a pastime. An automatic action. However stoned, they could all crumble softened hash into the hollowed tip of a straight or lick two Rizla papers together ready to be filled with loose tobacco rubbed with hash.

Visions were in the making. Half the clan was on acid. Four had touched Angel's Dust for the first time ever. Product of a Brooklyn backroom chemist's passionate experimentation, this was a body anaesthetic that blew the mind into a hallucinatory world an aeon on from acid. Five small crystals came in an envelope: *Smoke these!* some crazed head had written. They did. The rest watched. Tucked into the glowing tip of a king-size Marlboro filter, one puff each and the four were out. Far out. So far out there seemed no immediate certainty they'd ever get back – but, with their bodies immobilized, at least they were safe from physical damage. Two days later someone asked one of the four how his trip had been. Veteran of one hundred acid trips, shrugging, he shook his head in bewilderment. 'I don't know,' he said. 'Man, I just don't know.' This was the party the cops busted.

They came down out of the hills with their heavy boots crushing fresh bursts of scent out of the wild thyme and rosemary. It was an encircling operation, very military. Courageous considering the terrain. They arrived exhausted. Uniforms torn, hands and faces scratched, they burst into the fire-light. The flames danced over their sweat-glistening faces.

'Mother Acid – Hallelujah!' yelled a young gay kid from southern California and kissed the panting sergeant on the lips.

This was the warning. Hash hurtled into the fire – fresh incense for the mountainside. The moon winked and giggled; ducked out. The party relaxed. Who would arrest a hundred people with the island jail not big enough?

But the police took the gay kid. They had to. He refused to be left behind. And they handcuffed him, if only to keep him out of the sergeant's arms. And they busted Dutch Ned for riotous assembly without a permit. Not that he minded. He was leaving anyway at the end of the week. For the rest, the police collected names and passports while ordering the bearers to report to the station Monday morning. Then they left.

What with the police gone and the moon set, that was the party over. A half dozen stayed to help Dutch Ned's chick,

Ellen, clean up. Pleasure was one of these. Their only serious problem was where to store the four on Angel's Dust. The final choice was that of least resistance. They left them where they sat. A half ounce of Red Lebanese materialized from inside the rotten knot of an olive tree. With this for company, they waited round the embers of the dying fire.

Cape Kennedy Control. Around dawn the first of the four spacemen made it back from beyond the dark side of the moon; as yet not moving, there was enough happening in his eyes for them to tell he was home in his head. By ten that Sunday morning all four had achieved re-entry. Time to go.

The tin clatter of a bucket striking the cobbled street below his window jerked Pleasure awake. Eyes still closed, he grabbed for his denim pants – then he remembered he was free. Stretching voluptuously across the expanse of his outsize bed, he listened to the cathedral bells toll the hour. Monday morning. Ten o'clock. Opening his eyes, he rolled over to face the terrace.

She lay naked in the sun. She lay on her back with her feet pointing at the harbour. From the crest of her forehead her hair broke inland to flow like golden foam across the tiles. He could see her nose, the dark tips of her breasts, and then her toes. Her scent still trapped in the pillow beside him, he lay watching her – the infinitesimal rise and fall of her breasts. He moved his left leg so that the inside of his thigh bridged the slight hollow her body had left in the bed. He smiled ... slid out from under the sheet and walked silently on bare feet through to the kitchen where he opened the window.

'Manuela!' he shouted.

The washerwoman's daughter stuck her head out from the door across the streeet. She was fourteen years old. Nearly fifteen. Her hair was pitch black and her black eyes sparkled with mischief. In a year she would be a woman – beautiful, unless she let herself get fat as her mother had. Her mind was already similar.

'So,' she called. 'The great lover awakes.'

'And needs yoghurt for his strength,' Pleasure told her. 'Will you go to Maria's?'

'*Dos?*'

He grinned. '*Claro, niña.*'

'Copulator!'

'May I do nothing till you grow up?'

'Only practice,' she shouted back.

'You're too young to have such thoughts,' he told her.

'And if you continue in this manner you will be too old before I am old enough,' she warned.

'Go,' he told her. 'And hurry. You have a bad mind for one who is still a child.'

Laughing, she stuck out her tongue. 'How else can I be?' she asked. 'I who must clean your apartment. What I have seen in a week would destroy the soul of a saint.'

'As a saint you never had a chance. Go, or I will descend and chase you.'

'You have no trousers,' she guessed. 'Would you shame the *calle De La Virgen* with your nakedness?'

He shook his head in despair. 'Must I pray to you?'

'Prayers!' she jeered. 'Those I can obtain from the priests. My soul is theirs. My body is your concern.' She giggled. 'But I will bring you yoghurt that you may retain your strength.'

He watched her parade up the *calle*. Confident that he looked, she swung her ass. Her dress was thin cotton.

'Turn round,' Britta called from the terrace.

He laughed and did.

'Rat!'

He walked towards her.

'No,' she told him, 'you have to go to the police.'

Then she stretched, and smiled wickedly. 'Anyway I've had my money's worth. Five calls to Arlanda Airport. You've worked that off.'

Rising from the harbour edge, the old city of Ibiza is a pyramid of whitewashed houses on the crest of which stand the cathedral, the fortress and the Palacio Episcopal. Both the cathedral and the fortress are built of dressed sandstone, as are the city walls which loop the hill. Beneath these battlements is the fishermen's quarter – *La Pena* – a maze of unpaved alleys and cobbled stairways threading the cottages which lie piled like bleached shells washed up against the walls.

At eleven o'clock that sunny September day, a shaved and showered Pleasure stepped out from the stairway to his apartment. He stood still for a moment, blinking, waiting for his retinas to adapt to the light. With his right hand he adjusted his shades. This was habit – a polished gesture which drew a whistle from Pepita the washerwoman who sat on her front step two doors down.

'Hombre,' she called. 'Que guapo, hoy!'

True, he knew. He'd dressed with care and thought. He'd chosen a suit of blue-and-white striped lightweight Terylene. Washable, Pepita had starched its creases. The pale-blue shirt he wore was matched by a batik scarf. His blue canvas shoes were new. Cool, cool blue, he thought, as he dropped his shades to let fat Pepita catch his wink. He gave her a smile.

'*Gracias,*' he called, and turning, headed for the waterfront.

Just his passing seemed momentarily to conquer the heat. The neighbours smiled. A family of barefoot gypsy children danced in his train.

Having first collected his two-day-old *Tribune* from the bookshop next to police headquarters, Pleasure climbed the stairs to the waiting-room. There were ten other foreigners there. Pleasure nodded to the ones he knew.

Sitting down, he carefully adjusted his trouser legs before opening his paper at the cartoon page. This was his daily reading – Peanuts, BC and the Wizard of Id. Occasionally he also read the golf news, though he never knew why. He did so now. A longing for the security of the country club, he wondered, as the duty officer beckoned him into the inner office.

The police chief sat behind his desk. His hands toyed with a pile of passports. They were slim hands, white skinned and well cared for, with long delicate fingers.

'Buenos Dias, Señor Pleasure.' He half rose as he waved

Pleasure to the hard upright chair the wrong side of the desk. They sat looking at each other. The chief of police seemed almost sorrowful.

'Hardly professional,' he said.

'Professional?'

The chief nodded. 'Professional, Señor Pleasure.' He went back to inspecting the passports. Finally he shrugged. 'Such a small affair as a fiesta,' he murmured.

Pleasure had to lean forward to hear. Then he saw the letter. He couldn't read it. It was upside down. But he recognized the photograph fixed to the bottom. It was the duplicate from his first passport application. Twelve years . . . for the first time in his life Pleasure wished he'd aged.

'Was it a good fiesta?' the Spaniard asked.

'Fiesta?'

'Last night, Señor Pleasure.' The chief prodded. 'You were at a fiesta last night. You remember?'

Pleasure nodded. He tried desperately to think. Nothing came. He knew he was blushing. His penis itched. His hands were clammy with sweat. Then he shrugged. His voice was steady. 'There was no permission?' he asked.

'No. There was no permission,' the chief told him. 'Is it not sad, Señor Pleasure. Ten years you have been our guest. Never trouble. Always quiet. Always clean. Always polite.'

Silver-haired, a lined, jowled face with dark pouches under brown eyes, the elderly Spaniard looked like a doleful bloodhound. Only his hands gave him away. They were surgeon's hands, Pleasure thought. He watched them play with the passports.

'Sad,' the chief murmured again. *Triste, triste.* He shrugged. 'What can I do?' Eyebrows raised, he looked inquiringly at Pleasure.

Pleasure made no reply. The game was already lost. He had no wish to continue playing simply to amuse the Spaniard.

'This *is* yours?' the policeman asked.

He proferred a Canadian passport for Pleasure's inspection. Four and a half years old, the document was issued in the name of Isaac George Jacobson. The photograph showed a stern, bespectacled Pleasure wearing a striped tie and dark business suit. The passport had cost five hundred dollars. Pleasure glanced at it, nodded, then handed it back. The police chief placed it carefully on top of the letter.

'I am truly sorry,' he assured Pleasure. 'You understand? I must retain your document for a short while.'

Pleasure nodded. 'Sure,' he said. 'Anything you say, Don Ricardo.'

'You must believe me,' the chief pressed, 'truly I am sad.' He wrinkled his nose in distaste. 'You are not one of these dirty hippies, Señor Pleasure, and you have taken trouble to learn our language. We like you here. It is not we who make trouble for you ... ' he added quietly, his right hand indicating the letter on his desk. 'You understand?' he asked.

Pleasure nodded. 'I know,' he said. He had reached the door when the police chief called him back.

'Señor Pleasure ... '

Pleasure already had his hand on the brass knob. Now he turned. '*Sí*, Don Ricardo?'

'I must ask you a private question, joven. Will you answer me with truth?'

Now what was coming, Pleasure wondered, as he nodded.

'I know that you smuggle,' Don Ricardo told him quietly. 'That you have been till recently in prison. It was for hashish?'

Pleasure nodded again.

'That is all?' Don Ricardo asked. 'Never heroin or these whores of chemicals?'

'Never, Don Ricardo. I give you my word,' Pleasure assured the Spaniard. 'Never would I deal in such things!'

'I believe you.' For perhaps a minute the police chief sat lost in thought. He smiled. 'We also have military service,' he reminded Pleasure. 'Mine I spent in Morocco. We smoked *kief*,' he added with one eyebrow raised in self-mockery. 'That was a long time ago, and now I am chief of police. All of us smoked – the soldiers. Of the officers I know nothing.' He smiled again. 'Military service is not pleasant and for you Americans with

20

that obscenity of a war ... '

'It was a bad war, Don Ricardo.'

The Spaniard shrugged. 'It was a war without point,' he said. 'What penalties are exacted against those who refused their service?'

'Up to five years in prison, Don Ricardo.'

The Spaniard nodded slowly. 'A waste of a life,' he murmured.

For another minute he sat silently staring at the letter concerning the American. Finally he appeared to decide. Looking up, he said, 'We hear rumours from Madrid that your officials are not always correct in their behaviour concerning these matters. This is a small island, Señor Pleasure, we get to know each other well. The airport and the ferry-boats will be watched. I would not have you attempt to leave.' He shrugged and again his right hand flicked disdainfully at the report on his desk. 'For the moment there is no fear. Perhaps in a few days I will have more information. Then it is possible ... ' and he paused. Then he shrugged. 'If you have informed me with the truth, joven, then I will inform you in the evening of my desire to continue our investigation the following morning. You understand?' he asked.

Pleasure smiled. 'I believe I understand,' he said.

'Yes, you understand,' Don Ricardo answered him. 'Now you may go.' And he looked back down at his files and papers.

'Is it permitted for me to thank you?' Pleasure asked.

The Spaniard glanced up. 'It is not permitted,' he said. 'Gratitude is for assistance. I hope that you do not presume ... '

'Of course not, Don Ricardo,' Pleasure answered quickly. He saw the ghost of a smile flit over the Spaniard's face before he turned to open the door.

Standing on the corner of the *Avenida* and the *Vara Del Rey*, Pleasure watched the traffic. The municipal policeman on point duty gave him a smile which Pleasure returned. Ibiza, his home for ten years. One more goodbye. Still, things could be a lot worse, he thought, as he crossed the road and strolled on down the square. First job was to fix himself a ride off the island.

Ahead of him two large coaches had halted by the kerb. The doors were open. The tourists poured out on to the pavement where a guide stood marshalling them into some sort of order before marching them up through the old city.

Pleasure knew the guide. She was Swedish. Twenty-six years old. Summers she worked Ibiza, winters the Canary Islands. This morning she looked tired and a little bad tempered. It was a hot day for walking eighty people up the steep hill to the cathedral – eighty tourists who would ask the same questions as the previous eighty. They were always the same questions.

The tourists looked hot, pink, blistered and slightly bemused but happy. For a moment Pleasure envied them. They all had nice, safe jobs back home – except most of them probably hated their jobs. Pleasure waited till Brigitta had them moving, then he walked round the front of the lead coach. Papa Pedro sat up in the cab.

The old man had to be nearer seventy than sixty, Pleasure guessed. He'd owned two small 1928 Alfa Romeos when Pleasure had first come to the island. Now, with the tourist boom, he had six of these glass and aluminium monsters. But he still drove when he got the chance, he still wore the same faded blue overalls with thirty-inch bottoms, and he still always had the stump of a black *puro* sticking out of his mouth. He was Pleasure's landlord.

Reaching up, Pleasure banged on the windscreen. The Spaniard gave him a grin and a fist. 'Holá Palanquero,' the old man shouted down. *Palanquero* was the island word for some kind of Universal Copulator.

'I'm off,' Pleasure called up.

Papa Pedro shrugged. 'You'll be back.'

'I mean really off,' Pleasure told him.

The old man grinned. 'So I'll see you at my funeral,' he said. 'Till then I'll see whoever has your apartment keeps it clean.'

'I may be years,' Pleasure warned.

22

'Should I be in a hurry to die?' Papa Pedro asked.

Laughing, Pleasure thanked him, waved, then walked back to *La Pena*. A tall Afro-American in his late twenties lolled against the wall of Pepita's house. He wore faded blue jeans, a blue singlet and sandals. Whatever he'd just said to the washerwoman must have been highly indecent, Pleasure judged by the fat woman's delighted laughter.

'Quit perverting the natives,' Pleasure told Black Jack.

'Pervert Pepita – are you kidding?' Jack demanded.

The giant-breasted washerwoman had her tub out in the street. Black patches of sweat spread out of her armpits halfway down to her waist. Straightening up with a wet shirt in her hand, she used her forearm to push her hair back out of her eyes.

'Not bad for a Moor,' she told Pleasure with a jab of her thumb at Jack.

'You have to choose between us,' Pleasure warned.

'Between you!' she laughed. 'If I had both of you for breakfast I'd still be hungry.'

'Es un coño loco,' Pleasure told her. He pinched her ass – ducked as she slapped at him with the wet shirt.

'So what's new?' Jack asked as they reached the safety of Pleasure's studio.

Pleasure told him.

'Fuck!' Jack swore. 'Now what?'

Pleasure shrugged. 'Ride over to San Antonio and ask German George for a lift.'

While Ibiza City remains the capital of the Island, San Antonio is the tourist centre. More than twenty yachts lay stern-to along the quay and there were another dozen anchored out in the harbour. Siesta hour, there was neither a customs officer nor a port policeman on duty.

Pleasure strolled out along the quay. German George was a geologist. He'd worked fifteen years in Saudi Arabia, saved his money and retired.

Now he lived on a thirty-two-foot Nicholson sloop. She lay to a bow mooring with two crossed stern lines to the mole. The stern lines were joined by heavy-duty coil springs to the shackles which held them to the mooring rings set into the wall. Pleasure found the German sitting in his cockpit splicing a stainless-steel eye into the end of a length of nylon rope. George waved a bottle of beer at him. Pleasure dragged his boots off before stepping on board.

"Hi,' he said.

'Look in the ice box,' the German told him.

Pleasure went down below. The small saloon was spotless and warm with the colour and scent of teak. A chart of Ibiza and Formentera lay on the navigation table. He took a bottle of white wine out of the ice box, found the corkscrew in a galley drawer and a glass in the rack above the Simpson and Lawrence stove. These in hand, he joined George in the cockpit.

'I hear Dutch Ned got busted last night,' the German remarked as he watched Pleasure draw the cork. 'You there?'

Pleasure nodded. He poured himself a full glass then re-corked the bottle and put it away in the shade of the companion-way. He toasted the German. George was forty-six years old but looked a great deal younger. Stocky and heavily muscled, he had very pale grey eyes and short hair bleached almost white by the sun. He was the best sailor Pleasure had ever met. Impossible to panic, he found time to work out each move much as if sailing were a chess game. His yacht was always immaculate. Pleasure liked him a lot. He'd been family for seven years.

'I may need to get out of Spain,' he said.

George looked up at him. He didn't seem surprised. 'The police took your passport?' he asked.

Pleasure nodded. 'It wasn't mine,' he said and explained about the warning he expected to get from the chief.

George finished his beer while thinking. One of the tour boats which take holiday-makers out to the beaches bulled clumsily in past the end of the mole where it fell off the plane. The German watched its stern wave break against the square transsom before he turned back to Pleasure.

'Can you buy a new passport in France?' he asked.

'Paris,' Pleasure told him.

Opening one of the cockpit lockers, George put his empty beer bottle away in a carton, then he went below and came back up with a glass and a small-scale chart of the north-western Mediterranean. He gave Pleasure the chart to study while he filled his glass with wine.

'Somewhere close to Port Camargue would be best. Plenty of tourists,' he said. 'If I put you in on the beach, you can catch the bus to Arles. Further south and we'll be too close to the border – too many customs agents.' He sipped his wine and rolling the chart up, dropped it down on to the navigation table. 'You've got a minimum of four days' grace,' he said. 'I'll move over to Formentera tomorrow and lie in Es Palmador bay every night till you need me. Can you get someone to bring you over?'

Ed Palmador is a small island five miles from Ibiza harbour and separated from Formentera by eight hundred yards of shallows and sand banks. The island is privately owned and there are no police on it, the bay a safe anchorage in anything but a westerly gale.

Pleasure nodded. One of the fishermen would take him over. 'Thanks, George,' he said.

The German smiled and shrugged. 'Any time – it's all part of the family service.'

Five days till the police chief's warning came. Pleasure never saw who slipped the note under his door. He read it and burnt it. Britta was out on the terrace with Jack, Blind John, Jerry the Flute and an English girl called Jeannie. She had her leg in a cast on which Loved Graham had painted a wildly crumpled red Bultaco. The family, or part of the family. That's how they thought of themselves. There were other members spread all over the world. Some of them dealt dope. A few were in jail.

Britta caught Pleasure's eye. He nodded.

'What shall I pack?' she asked.

He looked round the studio. There were paintings on the

wall. Two he'd bought. The other three were gifts. Indian bronzes; his drums, tapes, records; the Braun record player and Akai tape deck; rugs he'd bought in Persia, Afghanistan and Kashmir; books, no photographs, the fan of red coral he'd pried loose from the reef off Eilat; two ebony masks from Senegal.

'Just clothes,' he said.

He took down the two American Touristers from the top of the closet and laid them open on the bed. The cases were ready prepared. They held four kilos each.

He stood watching Britta pack for a while then he went out and down the *calle* to where one of the fishermen lived. He knocked on the open door. 'Pep?'

'Si, hombre.' The fisherman waved him in. 'Qué quieres?'

'I have to get to Es Palmador,' Pleasure told him.

Pep did not look surprised. 'Tonight?'

Pleasure nodded. 'I have trouble.' he said 'Police.'

Pepe grinned. 'Who does not?' he asked. Meaning himself and the other fishermen, many of whom were smugglers on the side 'You have baggage?'

'Two cases.'

The Spaniard thought for a moment. 'I will bring my handcart. We hide your belongings below the nets, then I must leave the harbour by myself.'

'The beach below the castle?' Pleasure suggested.

Pepe nodded. He looked at his watch. 'The moon will rise at three. Half-past twelve?'

'Gracias, Pep.'

'De nada, hombre. Hasta mas tarde.'

'Which way are you heading?' Black Jack asked.

'Paris – then East.' Pleasure told him.

'Going to make a run?'

Pleasure shrugged. 'What else?' he asked. He handed Jack the keys and papers for his bike. Going out to the terrace, he carried in the two chairs, the table and the sun mattresses. This done, he closed the windows and locked them. He collected his crocodile-skin brief-case from the closet.

'That's about it,' he said. He smiled ruefully as he took a last look round the studio. Gave the keys to Jack.

'I told Papa Pedro I was off,' he said. 'He told me to keep the pad. That means we can sub-let like before.'

Jack nodded. 'And the bread for your bike?' he asked.

For a moment Pleasure hesitated. Then he shrugged. 'Keep it till Christmas.'

'Goa?'

'Right,' Pleasure said.

'If you're not in jail,' Jack warned.

Pleasure shrugged again. 'Let's go eat,' he said.

CHAPTER TWO

Patrick John Nolan managed a grunt of acquiescence in answer to the loud knocking on his bedroom door. He'd been sleeping curled up in a tight question mark with his hands clasped between his thighs. Yawning, he stretched out and half opened his eyes to watch the elderly waiter carry his breakfast tray over to the desk in the bow window which overlooked the Bosphorus.

The Turk gave Patrick a warning nod before reaching for the curtains. Patrick looked the other way. Even with his back to the window, the bright sunlight hurt his eyes – and why should the roots of his hair ache, he wondered, as he watched the waiter disappear into the bathroom where he opened both faucets. A second nod to Patrick and the old man left.

Turks! Struggling out from under the bedclothes, Patrick swung his feet to the carpet and sat coughing while the room steadied. Each cough triggered two small hammers rigged behind his eyes. Collecting his orange juice from the tray, he carried the glass through to the bathroom where he added two Alka Seltzer. By the time he'd bathed, shaved and brushed his teeth, he felt able to face breakfast – not the food, but coffee and his first cigarette. He drank his coffee black. Two cups and he was ready to dress. He selected a white shirt, blue socks, black shoes and a blue suit. The tie he chose bore a neat bold anchor motif. It looked like a club tie. Perhaps it was. But not his club. He'd neither joined nor been asked to join a club in his life.

Dressed, he checked his image in the full-length mirror by the door. He was six feet tall, slim but reasonably muscled. His hair was black and naturally wavy and his eyes were a

28

spaniel brown. A firm chin thrust forward under a mouth which was surprisingly gentle considering the strength of his jaw and cheek-bones. Deep ravines flared out each side of a thin, aquiline nose. These trenches, together with his eyes, gave him a permanent look of slight melancholy and self-doubt.

Third-generation Irish American, twenty-eight years old, Patrick was an employee of the Department of Justice, Bureau of Narcotics and Dangerous Drugs. Normally he was a resident of Frankfurt, Germany. He'd been in Istanbul a week. A few more days and he could go home – if his sterile studio apartment in Frankfurt could be considered a home. Originally he'd planned to drive back to Germany with one of the consular staff. This was now impossible since cholera in eastern Turkey had given Greeks and Bulgarians an excuse to close their frontiers.

Turkey was the first truly impoverished country Patrick had ever visited. He did not count Vietnam. He knew he should but could not. He'd never known with the Vietnamese: neither what they wanted, nor how nor what they felt. That had been the American sin, he thought now, as he strolled down through Bebek towards the consulate ... not the bombing, but the famine of comprehension from which grew inhumanity till finally the Vietnamese became immaterial – so immaterial that American protest had been concerned not with the fact of the Vietnamese being bombed but that it was they, the Americans, who dropped the bombs. *Mea culpa, Mea culpa, Mea maxima culpa*, Patrick murmured, as he crossed the streeet.

He nodded to the two policemen on duty outside the gates. A crowd of kids swamped the consulate lobby – forty or fifty of them with more outside in the garden. Most were male: long-haired freaks wearing odd scraps of Eastern clothing along with their Levis and sandals. A few were here for their mail. The rest were demanding news of the borders. They all seemed so anbry, Patrick thought, as he caught a glimpse of a harried-looking vice-consul barricaded in behind the reception counter.

Back to the wall, Patrick edged round the crowd to the safety of his own office. A low pile of brown-covered files lay on the right-hand corner of his desk. There was a second and much taller stack on the window-sill. Those by the window he'd already checked. He'd finish the remainder in two days at the most he hoped, then back to the equal monotony of Frankfurt.

Sighing as he sat down, he pulled the top file down and opened it. These were Turkish police records: dull lists of border crossings – names, dates, vehicle registration numbers – so dull he'd had to come to Istanbul to check them. No Turkish clerk would bother – and why should they, Patrick mused. He hadn't much enthusiasm himself.

In the years prior to 1969, an estimated eighty per cent of all opium-based narcotics smuggled into the States originated here in Turkey. Now, through a system of bribes and subsidies, the U.S. had persuaded the Turkish authorities to outlaw poppy cultivation. The poppy still got grown of course, but now the farmers had to plant corn as camouflage plus being forced to bribe the local law.

During the legal days of opium production, the Turkish dealers had been helpfully casual. Tracing the raw product through to the French heroin laboratories had been comparatively easy – not that this tracing had helped. The Marseilles labs had been well protected and the idea of an American narcotics agent receiving co-operation from the French police, particularly under a Gaullist regime, had been sadly ludicrous. Now, with cultivation illegal, the Turks were more circumspect, which made the Bureau's task increasingly difficult rather than easier. Not that this mattered much, Patrick mused, as he plodded on with his search. Whatever the Bureau did, the heroin still got through. Corruption back home saw to that.

He worked steadily, if without much enthusiasm, till eleven o'clock, when his door opened and Ken Kennedy came in. The forty-year-old vice-consul was built like a bull. He had short sandy-red hair, bright-blue eyes and a stubborn mouth. Now he looked tired, hot, ill-tempered and disgusted.

'Jesus, those kids!' he cursed as he parked half his ass on the corner of Patrick's desk. Dragged by the way he sat, the single button of his wash-and-wear jacket looked ready to fly. 'They make me so damned mad,' he complained.

Patrick said nothing. There was no point.

'Patsies – that's us,' Ken said after a while. 'Catholic Patsies for their God-damned Jewish hang-ups.' He undid the tight button with thick strong fingers more suitable for a prize fighter than a consul. 'They hate oguts,' he grumbled. 'Temporary father substitutes they can work their God-damned hate out on till they get home. Is it my fault the border's closed?' he demanded.

Pulling a crumpled pack of Camels from his breast pocket, he offered one to Patrick. The first match he struck broke. The flarinb head dropged on to his gants, then to the floor. Ken stamped it out. 'Not my day,' he said. 'God-damned kids! Know something?' he asked. 'They smile. Like they ask some incredible question I can't answer, right? And when I can't answer, they *smile*. It's like they believe we're deliberately shafting them and they're pleased. See what I mean? Us shafting them proves we're bastards.' He almost spat that last word. Then he took a deep drag on his cigarette, blew the smoke out and sat studying the glowing tip of the Camel for a while before turning back to look down at Patrick again.

'Look – if they hate us so God-damned much,' he said, 'then why in hell do they have to come running every time they have a problem? That's what pisses me – they're so God-damned inconsistent.' He blew more smoke. 'You want coffee?' he asked.

Patrick nodded. More comprehension famine, he thought, as he watched the broad-backed vice-consul bull his way out of the small office as if it were a pen. Ken Kennedy had his true-blue All American indignation. The kids had their belief that dope and Eastern mysticism made them the chosen of God. Total barrier! That, plus Ken being overworked with having had to drive twice to the border in the last three days.

'You want me to stand in as duty officer tonight?' he asked, when the vice-consul came back in with the coffee. 'Give you a break.'

'That would be great,' Ken said.

The telephone rang at ten minutes past two in the morning. Patrick had the last file but three open on the desk beside the switchboard. A cup of coffee stood steaming by his elbow. He enjoyed isolation – always had – and he lifted the receiver reluctantly. 'American Consulate,' he said.

'Light,' a boy's voice whispered down the line. 'Light,' the voice pleaded. 'I must have light.' Then the line went dead.

Patrick lowered the receiver and sat staring at it for almost a minute before his mind worked. He called the police. He was still trying to break through the language barrier when the boy called for the second time. Again that whispered cry for light.

'Where are you?' Patrick interrupted. 'You've got to tell me where you are.'

Nothing.

Patrick sat angrily shaking the receiver as if some clue might fall out of the black Bakelite cup while on the other line the police operator jabbered on at him.

Closing out the operator, Patrick dialled Allbright, the junior vice-consul who spoke Turkish. Rapidly he explained his need to have all incoming calls traced. That done, he had nothing to do but wait.

Jack Allbright joined him within the half hour. He'd called the police. He was quick: that was the best one could say for him, Patrick thought, watching the rumple-suited vice-consul stride up and down the lobby. He had an irritating habit of pawing at his scalp.

'For Christ's sake sit down,' Patrick finally snapped. The phone rang. The police. They had a dead American student in a hotel room over by the Blue Mosque. Suicide. Patrick took the address.

The hotel was a dump. Two policemen waited in the lobby along with the manager. Dressed in baggy white pyjamas, the manager was grey-faced and scared. There was a big dark stain on the ceiling directly over his couch. That's what had wakened him, he said. The blood dripping.

Patrick found the officer upstairs in the boy's room. The Turk nodded a brief greeting and held out his hand to show Patrick four small tabs of pink-stained paper cupped in a scrap of silver foil. LSD, Patrick guessed. Proof would come with the lab report.

The boy lay on the bed with his head lolling back over the edge and one hand flung out towards the telephone which sat on a side-table just beyond his reach. The wrist cuts had done no harm. Instead of up the artery, the boy had cut straight across. That way it was difficult to get depth.

But the neck job was thorough. The deep gash gaped open with the severed ends of the carotid artery plainly visible. Blood had sprayed all down one wall as well as over the bed and the floor.

The corpse looked so deserted, Patrick thought. He stepped gingerly forward to check arms and ankles. There was no way he could avoid getting blood on his shoes. He saw no needle marks so the boy had not even been a junkie. Blond, blue-eyed, he'd been a good-looking kid, fine faced and slim, with slender hands. One bad acid trip and now someone would have to call his mother. Kennedy's job, Patrick thought; he turned and picked up a two-day-old *Tribune* which lay folded open at the funnies on the side-table beside the telephone. Carrying the paper out into the corridor, he stood staring at the Wizard of Id for a while, then shrugged and, bending down, used the paper to wipe his shoes.

The men from the city morgue shuffled past him into the boy's room. He watched them roll the body on to a canvas stretcher. Followed them downstairs. The manager was gone, as were the two policemen. Alone and waiting for the officer, he stood reading the scrawled messages pinned to a small board on the wall by the door.

$30 Kabul. Leaving Tuesday. Contact Jack. Room 8.

Free ride for two chicks. VW camper heading East

Friday. Mike and Ray, Room 1, Hotel Aya Sofya

TEHERAN – KABUL – LAHORE – DELHI –
KATMANDU. Bus leaves Monday. Contact driver.
BLUE MOSQUE CAR PARK, Grey Bedford XKL
22451

The Dope Trail, Patrick mused and turned to meet the police
officer at the foot of the stairs. 'Find anything?' he asked.

'Hashish.' The officer shrugged. Handed Patrick the boy's
passport. 'Five grams. Nothing.'

'Will I get to see the lab report?' Patrick asked.

The officer nodded. 'Tomorrow,' he promised. 'Want a lift?'

Patrick shook his head. 'I'm in no hurry,' he said.

They shook hands at the Turk's car. The sky was frost clear
and a slight breeze tugged gently at Patrick's trouser legs and
at the tail of his topcoat. Cradled in a doorway behind him, a
bundle of rags stirred restlessly, coughed twice, hawked and
spat. A sheet of newspaper blew across the road, caught on the
kerb, then lifted and scuttled on over the pavement and across
the square towards the Blue Mosque. Cars, coaches and
campers stood in untidy rows. A blue Volkswagen with German
tourist plates caught Patrick's eyes. The camper looked
showroom-fresh except for the red Om painted on its side. A tin
cocoon. The mobile ghetto readied for its winter migration
East. White sand. Palm trees. Freedom. A few deaths.
Frankfurt. Concrete. The bundle of rags coughed. Patrick
looked down. A pebble lay on the pavement. His foot shot
forward. The pebble struck the camper. Proving what, Patrick
wondered. He turned left and walked slowly down the hill to
the Golden Horn.

The Galata Bridge was open. He strolled out to the edge of
the gap. He could hear the rhythmic thump of single-cylinder
diesels pushing upstream towards the bridge ... heavy heart-
beats. At what stage of his acid trip had the boy called the
consulate? Had his wrists been already bleeding, Patrick
wondered, watching the bright lights of a liner creep in towards
the deep-water quay. A convoy of four caiques thrust their way

through the gap in the bridge. It had been their diesels he'd heard. The boats were moon crescents of mountain pine and the scent of freshly mown alfalfa drifted up from their laden decks. They passed. The bridge closed. A hopeful cabby U-turned. Patrick flagged him.

A bag had arrived from Washington. Jack Allbright sat sorting the mail while an early-morning cleaner slopped water over the tiled floor.

'Bad?' he asked.

Patrick nodded. He fetched two cartons of coffee from the dispenser, then went through to his own office. There was a half-full bottle of Ballantine's in the bottom drawer of his desk. He took a quick gulp neat before carrying it out to where Allbright sat. He added stiff tots to their coffees, then took out a pack of Marlboro.

'Smoke?' he offered.

The vice-consul took one. 'There's a letter for you,' he said
. . .

From the Bureau, Patrick saw, as he slit the envelope. A photograph fell out.

ROBERT JACOB GOLDBERG ALIAS *PLEASURE*
Born New York City – February 11th, 1943. First arrest December 25th, 1960 – jumped bail. Arrested Flensburg, Denmark – December 17th, 1971 in possession of 40 kilos hashish. Sentenced twenty-eight months' imprisonment. Released September 17th, 1973 for repatriation.
Escaped custody Copenhagen Airport.
Flew Geneva on American passport issued in name of George Katz.
Traced Ibiza, Spain, September 28th, on Canadian passport in name of Gerald Arthur Cohen.
Evaded arrest.
Seen Paris October 6th.
Now believed heading East.
Evidence at 1971 trial together with effectiveness of

35

escape methods show membership of well organized drug ring.

Subject can be expected to be dangerous.

Jack Allbright had picked up the photograph. 'Could almost be your twin,' he said.

The express from Rome reached Naples at half past three in the afternoon. Pleasure carried his own bags off the train. He checked they were locked, booked them in at the baggage counter, then left the station and walked up the Corso Garibaldi as far as Via Foria. He window-shopped. Twice he stopped abruptly, only to backtrack hurriedly for twenty or thirty paces as if he'd left something behind. He crossed and recrossed the street and finally grabbed a cab outside the entrance to the Botanical Gardens. He told the driver to circle round to the side entrance of the station. Here he paid the cabby his fare plus a dollar and asked him to wait.

Walking back through the station he found a travel agency. There was no boat to the Lebanon for six days but there was a ship leaving that night for Istanbul. The American bought a second-class ticket. Though there were four berths in the cabin, this was not the tourist season and the agent doubted if he'd have to share. The American was not worried. Five dollars to the purser would buy privacy.

He bought a *Tribune,* collected his bags, then returned to his cab. There were no other cabs on the street and no parked car with a driver waiting behind the wheel. Satisfied, he told the cabby to drop him at the Majestic.

Getting out at the hotel, he had a porter carry his bags into the lobby. He over-tipped the man, then crossed to the corner telephone kiosk where he spent nearly five minutes involved in an imaginary conversation. Both the receptionist and the head-porter were watching him as he came back to the desk. Smiling apologetically, he asked how he could get to Positano. The receptionist looked up trains. One left at six o'clock that evening for Castellamare from where, he was told, he should hire a car to take him up over the mountains.

Thanking the receptionist profusely, Pleasure tipped him heavily. Satisfied he would be remembered, he had himself driven back to the station where he spent fifteen minutes over a cup of coffee and his newspaper. Then he took a cab directly to the docks. On the way he studied his latest passport. George Katz had been good only for the Geneva flight. Mister Cohen remained with the authorities in Spain. This new document he'd bought in Paris was British. It had eleven weeks remaining, which was bad. On the other hand he'd bought it cheap and quick and he knew he could easily obtain a fresh one in Istanbul.

Five days to Istanbul. Pleasure ate a leisurely breakfast before disembarking. He had no trouble with his passport – nor did he have any problems at the customs bench. He booked his bags into a small hotel in the Yenikoy district before catching a cab down to the Galata Bridge. Crossing on foot, he walked uphill towards the Blue Mosque – the Sultan Ahmed quarter – a district of run-down and never-come-up hotels and lodging houses, of bad restaurants and worse cafés. There were a lot of young Westerners about. Freaks.

Pleasure turned right at the top of the hill and ducked down a narrow alley.

A small restaurant faced him. The tables were scrubbed pine – only five – and there were benches along the walls. The room was empty.

Pleasure stuck his head through the serving hatch. 'Hi,' he called.

The middle-aged Turk by the stove turned and immediately smiled. 'Pleasure!' he cried. 'Where you been?'

Pleasure smiled back. 'Jail,' he admitted. 'Copenhagen.'

Sorrowfully, the Turk shook his head then reached for the kettle. 'Tea?'

That was Pleasure's first stop. He made three more and was on his way to the fifth when he spotted a young Turk on the other side of the road. Their eyes met above the traffic. A quick nod from Pleasure indicated to the Turk that he should follow. The American walked on for a quarter of a mile before turning in to a café crowded with students from the university. He found an empty table against the back wall, sat down and ordered two coffees. He had already been served by the time the Turk slid into the seat across the table.

'Hi, Ishmid,' Pleasure said as he pushed over the second cup. 'How's business?'

'Not bad,' Ishmid told him.

In his mid twenties, the Turk was dressed neatly in grey trousers and a tweed jacket. The roll-necked jersey he wore looked as though it came from Ireland.

'And the chicks?' the American asked.

Ishmid smiled. His teeth were good and his dark eyes laughed. Taking out his wallet, he passed the American a bad photograph of what could have been a pretty blonde. The girl wore jeans and a sweater similar to the one Ishmid wore.

'Irish?' Pleasure asked.

Ishmid nodded. 'Here all summer,' he boasted proudly.

The American watched the Turk sip his coffee. In the end you always had to trust someone, he thought.

'Can I score?' he asked quietly.

Ishmid looked up over the lip of his cup. The cobwebs of humour at the corners of his eyes were suddenly gone. He took a packet of flat Turkish cigarettes out of his jacket pocket, offered one to the American, lit them both.

'Hash?' he asked.

Pleasure nodded.

'How many kilos?'

'Eight,' Pleasure told him. 'Top quality.'

'How soon?'

'I'm short on time,' Pleasure said.

'And you want hash not *kima*.'

They both smiled. Used by the Turks to mark their sheep, *kima* was a type of henna with much the same colour and texture as pressed cannabis pollen.

'No,' Pleasure agreed. 'I don't want *kima*.'

38

'They fooled a German last month,' Ishmid told him. 'Eighty kilos in a VW. The Greek customs got him at the border and the whole lot was *kima*.'

The American chuckled. 'That's one man who's glad he got ripped,' he said. 'You still in the business?'

Ishmid shook his head. 'Sometimes for friends,' he said. 'But it's dangerous and small profit. Now I do travellers' cheques.'

'Buying them?'

The Turk grinned. 'If I can't steal them,' he admitted. 'I pay forty per cent for unsigned cheques,' he explained. 'Then I sell them in the market for fifty-five.' He shrugged. 'Passports too. Junkies. They sell everything.'

'Who fixes the photographs?' Pleasure asked.

Ishmid looked up at him. 'You need a passport?' he asked.

'If it's a good one,' Pleasure told him. 'How much?'

'Two fifty with your own picture.'

The American took out his wallet. He had a small packet of passport portraits for visas. Slipping one out, he flicked it across the table.

'American?' Ishmid asked.

'Canadian would be better,' Pleasure told him. 'You want bread in advance?'

'Fifty,' Ishmid told him. 'I have to pay the man who fixes the picture.'

The American nodded. 'And the dope?' he asked.

Ishmid thought for a moment. 'Tonight,' he said. 'Nine o'clock here. I give you the passport and tell you about the hash.'

'Good.' Getting up, the American shook Ishmid's hand. The Turk palmed the fifty, smiled and was gone.

Sitting there that evening in the same café Pleasure sipped coffee and watched the door. He was ten minutes early for the rendezvous. Two tables down, four students played dice with match-boxes. Every three throws produced a loser whose hand the others grabbed and whopped shit out of with an empty Coke bottle – which about summed Turkey up, the American

39

thought. There were no winners, and no victories – the best you could hope for was that this wouldn't be your turn to get hit. Which brought him back to Ishmid.

How well did he know the Turk, he wondered. He'd drunk coffee with him a few times on each of his previous visits to the city. And he'd had friends who'd scored through him. But in summer. Summer was safer. There was more money around. Not quite the same necessity to rob . . . which was where trust was at, he thought now as he watched Ishmid slip in through the door. Seeing him, the Turk came slowly across the long room, not shoving, giving no offense, making himself unobtrusive. That was professional enough, Pleasure thought. He smiled at Ishmid, giving him his hand.

'Okay?' he asked.

Ishmid nodded. His eyes didn't seem over-anxious for contact, but he tapped his pocket.

Looking over to the bar, Pleasure signalled the waiter. 'What do you want?' he asked. 'Coffee?'

'*Raki*,' Ishmid told him. He rubbed his hands together against the cold outside. 'Bad winter coming,' he said.

'You want coffee too?' Pleasure asked. Talk of a bad winter made him uneasy. He wished to hell Ishmid would look him in the eye.

The Turk shook his head. 'A large *raki*,' he said.

He waited for the waiter to leave before slipping an envelope out of his jacket and across to the American.

Pleasure put it in his pocket, stood up and went into the john. Door locked, he took the packet out. It was an American passport in the name of Lester Schultz. The photograph was perfect and the brief had three years to run.

Back at the table, he smiled.

'Great,' he said. He had two one-hundred-dollar bills in his hand, which he palmed to the Turk.

'Junkie?' he asked.

Ishmid nodded.

'Think he's got a record?'

Ishmid shrugged. 'He say no,' he told the American. Which,

they both knew, was what the junkie would say however badly he was wanted.

'And the hash?' the American asked.

'Fixed,' Ishmid said, but his eyes were all over the place.

Maybe he was just nervous, Pleasure thought. He'd produced a good brief.

'When?' he asked.

'Tonight. Eleven o'clock.'

'Where?'

'Car park by the Blue Mosque.'

For a moment their eyes met.

'There's two buses,' the Turk told him. 'English buses. Between them at eleven o'clock. Good shit,' he added. 'And no danger. There's a guard.'

The American nodded. 'Do you get a cut?' he asked.

When Ishmid shook his head, Pleasure reached for his money.

'No,' Ishmid told him. 'I have enough with the passport.'

Guilt, the American wondered, as he watched the Turk finish his drink.

'Sure?' he asked.

Ishmid nodded. 'I have to go,' he said.

Again there was a brief moment when their eyes met. Too brief. But it was like he'd thought that morning, Pleasure decided. You had to trust someone. Their hands touched and the Turk was up.

'See you,' he said.

So now he was Lester Schultz, Pleasure thought, watching Ishmid thread his way out through the crowd. Lester Schultz, born New York City, November 20th, 1945. A Scorpio. He sat there sipping his coffee and wondering how many grains of morphine his new brief represented. Enough to keep the poor *mother* out of pain for a week? A month? He could remember the excitement he'd felt when he'd bought his first false identity. He'd just skipped bail back home. He'd felt adventurous – somehow important – like a false passport was a status symbol. Now he just felt old. Old and tired. This had to be the end. Eight kees. Where should he sell them, he wondered? Amsterdam in safety for seven hundred dollars a kee, Copenhagen for a thousand, or Canada for two? But he daren't risk Canada. Lester Schultz could be hot. And if he went down again in Scandinavia he'd be in bad trouble. Amsterdam it was. Five thousand five hundred dollars after expenses . . . and then what?

He'd like to go home, he suddenly admitted. Fly straight into Kennedy, clean. Rent a car. Drive out to Greenwich. Ring the bell. Who'd open the door, he wondered? His mother, his father or the maid? Probably the maid. They were into that trip – not that he cared any more. All he wanted to do was sit in a big, fat chair in front of the fire and rest. Bob Goldberg . . . it wasn't so bad a name after all.

He took a pad out of the bag he'd brought to carry the dope, and his pen from his inside jacket pocket.

Dear Mom (he wrote)
I'm sorry not to have written for so long. Seems crazy –
here I am in Istanbul again and where I'd really like to be
is back home . . .

Looking up, he caught the waiter's eye. He ordered another coffee and, as an afterthought, a large *raki*. The *raki* he drank neat – one swallow. As the alcohol exploded against the bottom of his belly, a fireball swept up through his body. He sat there rocked for a moment. Looked down at the letter he'd started. ' . . . *only I can't come home,*' he wrote. Then he crumpled the sheet of paper up and dropped it in the ashtray. Looking at his watch, he saw he had an hour to wait. Taking out his wallet, he counted his money: eight hundred and thirty dollars left, plus twenty in Turkish lira. He took out five hundreds and three twenties as well as the lira. The dollars were to pay for the dope. He folded these away into his breast pocket. The lira he put in his sock, the wallet and his new passport into the envelope Ishmid had given him. Picking up his bag, he went over to the bar, paid, then walked downhill to the little restaurant which had been his first stop that morning.

He walked on the right-hand side of the street – the dark side along by the car park. He could see the buses. The guard was on duty – an old man in an outsize topcoat. He had a brass badge on his breast and a wooden club in his hand. Should be safe, the American thought. Maybe paranoia was a by-product of jail.

Crossing over at the intersection, he walked down the short alley into the restaurant. There was an empty table by the door. The waiter came over. Pleasure ordered a bowl of mutton stew and a yoghurt. He was halfway through his first course when the owner came out of the kitchen. The Turk saw him, smiled and came over. The American slid along the bench to give him room.

'So what's happening?' the Turk asked as he sat down.

'Not much,' Pleasure told him. 'Maybe I'll leave tomorrow.'

'Better,' the Turk said. He sounded worried.

The American took another spoonful of stew before turning to look at the restaurateur. 'What's up?' he asked.

'Someone looks for you,' the Turk told him. 'American. He has a picture. Here, Pudding Shop, hotels.'

Pleasure pushed his food away. He had a tight bad feeling in his belly.

'Police?' he asked.

The Turk shrugged. 'Possible,' he said. 'Look like you – younger maybe. Suit, short hair, no beard.'

Pleasure took out the envelope containing his passport and wallet.

'Look after these,' he asked as he slid the packet across. 'I'll drop by in the morning.'

The Turk nodded. For a moment his hand squeezed the American's arm.

'Good luck,' he murmured and looked away quickly as if embarrassed.

'*In-sh'allah*,' Pleasure told him as he got up. Then he smiled. 'See you,' he said.

The Turk nodded. 'Take care,' he begged, and went back into the kitchen.

43

Pleasure paid the waiter. Outside, he found it was raining – not hard, but enough, and bitterly cold. He took his mac out of the bag. Buttoned up to his throat, with his collar turned up, he looked at his reflection in a shop window. He looked like a spy in a bad movie – 007, he thought. Only he didn't have a gun. Never had a gun. Hated them. He glanced at his watch. Three minutes.

He crossed over and circled the car park so as to come into it from the Mosque end. A man waited between the two buses. He had a cardboard box by his feet. There didn't seem to be anyone else about.

'Hi,' Pleasure said.

The Turk nodded. His hands were empty. He looked to be around the same age as Ishmid. He wore a fur hat folded down over his ears.

'It's there,' he said. He pointed down at the box.

The American squatted quickly. Opened the box. The shit was in half-pound slabs and not wrapped. He stuck his nose in. It was hash all right. Good quality by the smell and feel.

The Turk blew his nose loudly. Pleasure thought he heard someone move behind him. And he suddenly realized that he hadn't seen the guard. Then the cosh hit him. As he pitched forward a boot thudded into his ribs.

He didn't know how long he'd been out. He came to with the guard kneeling over him. The old man had a piece of rag in his hand with which he attempted to clean the American's face. Pleasure tried to get up. He got as far as sitting, then the sky and the buses started to spin together till he couldn't tell which was what. He was cold as hell and the buttons had been ripped off his mac. Blinking the world straight, he looked down at his watch. No watch. He felt his breast pocket. No money.

The guard was talking away. He looked scared. Pleasure wondered how they'd got rid of the old man. Given him a lira to get himself a cup of coffee. Poor old motherfucker – there was no point in blaming him. Using the side of one bus, Pleasure pushed himself up. The Turk held him. Pleasure wondered how bad he looked. Taking the rag from the guard, he did his best to clean his face. Then he took off his ruined mac. He stuffed that back in his bag. Bending down nearly put him out again. His lira were still in his sock. He gave a one to the guard and heard the old man mumbling thanks. Picking up his bag he walked slowly out of the car park and down the street to the baths. His head felt like hell and he looked like hell, he saw in each lighted window he passed. The last thing he wanted was to get stopped by a cop.

The *hamam* door was open. He walked across the entrance court and into the reception. Behind the desk sat a big, fat half-asleep Turk with a towel round his waist and his tits spilling down over his belly. Pleasure gave him the equivalent of a dollar. The Turk took a key off the board, picked up Pleasure's bag and led him upstairs to the changing-rooms.

'Tea?' he asked.

Pleasure didn't answer. He was looking at himself in the mirror. Even under the smeared-in dirt he could see streaks of dead-white face. He looked like he was about to go down again. He raised his right hand to the back of his head. Looked at his fingers. They were red and sticky. The bump was split right open.

Then the Turk started to curse. He didn't seem to have taken in how the American looked till he saw the blood. Now he pushed Pleasure down on to the bed and screamed orders down the stairs. Pleasure was surprised how gentle the fat man's fingers felt as the Turk examined the cut. His head nodded forward against the Turk's belly. He didn't have the strength to get it back up. Then he smelt Dettol. A boy had come into the room. Cotton wool dabbed at his head – cotton wool soaked in warm disinfectant. The sting cleared his eyes. His right side hurt like hell and was already stiffening. He wondered how many times they'd put in the boot. And why? The cosh seemed reasonable – at least it was a means to an end. The boot was gratuitous. Evil, he thought, as he tried to get his jacket off.

The bath attendant helped him. Moving his right arm sent stabs of pain down his side so that he gasped and his eyes watered. The shirt was easy. He unbuttoned it himself; the

Turk peeled it down his back – which left his T-shirt. He lifted the right side with his left hand. Dark blue with orange traces covered half his rib-cage. Again the fat man was shouting. This time the boy brought a cut-throat razor.

The Turk gave the American a woeful smile; cut delicately up through the side of the T-shirt, down the arm, and then the neckband. For a moment he looked at the bruises. Then he cut up the other side of the shirt. He threw the two halves on to the floor. Kneeling down, he untied the American's shoes and took off his socks. Pleasure undid his belt. Standing up with the attendant's help, he got his trousers and pants down. The Turk wrapped a towel round the American's waist then helped him downstairs and into the baths.

The heat and humidity seemed a physical barrier. The atmosphere was religious. No noise. No speech. A centre dome curved above a raised pentagon of marble on which lay five bodies. Two looked to be Westerners. Separated from the main dome by filigreed screens of butter-coloured marble were four smaller domes. Everything was marble – the floor of black-and-white slabs; the creamy pillars which supported the junction of the great and lesser domes; the white walls. Halfway between each of the corner enclosures stood big black clam shells from which water splashed on to the step and then ran off through grid holes in the floor.

The attendant spread a fresh towel on the raised pentagon, folding a second into a low pillow to protect the American's head. Lying there with the heat melting up through the marble into his body, Pleasure had a chance to think out his new position. He had two hundred dollars left and nowhere to go. As simple as that, he thought. No money and no future. The trouble with the dope business was not its danger but that it got to be a habit. Once you'd been in the business as long as he had, there wasn't much else you could do. That was the fascination of the hundred-kilo number – a big chunk of capital was your only way out. That or a job on the roads.

The attendant returned bearing a cup of hot mint tea and two codeines. Pleasure smiled his gratitude and swallowed the pills. His pores were opening and the sweat had begun to run. The fat Turk knelt beside him, huge hands kneading the American's body. He seemed capable of concentrating the whole of his gross weight into the tips of his fingers. There was no possibility of resistance. Pleasure lay comatose – his mind drifting free of his body so that it was almost a corpse which the Turk squeezed and pummelled. He knew every joint and each muscle, and he knew instinctively the exact point at which pressure would turn to pain. This was the barrier on the edge of which he worked. Not once did he hurt Pleasure – not even when his hands moved up over the American's right side. Finally he was satisfied. Rocking back on to his heels, he sat sweating rivers and smiling.

'Tea?' he asked, his voice a low whisper.

Pleasure moved his head a quarter of an inch to signal assent. The masseur raised a finger to the boy squatting by the door.

'Man, you really get service.' The voice came from behind Pleasure's head. Canadian, he guessed.

Then, 'Jesus!' the same voice swore, but now from beside him.

Pleasure opened his eyes. One of the two Westerners had moved over to look at him. Now he'd seen Pleasure's side.

'What the fuck happened to you?' he asked.

He had bright-blue eyes in a round face with prominent cheek-bones. His hair was the colour of fresh straw. He looked to be about twenty-two.

'I made a mistake,' Pleasure told him quietly.

He didn't want to talk. The Canadian's voice had been loud, the words echoing back off the smooth dome overhead.

'Some mistake,' he said. 'Truck or boot?'

Pleasure smiled weakly. 'Boot,' he admitted. 'I got ripped.'

'Fuck. Which way you headed?'

Pleasure tried to shrug. Keeping his eyes open was too much effort. So was talking. But he wasn't to be allowed that easy an escape.

'Been East?' the Candadian asked. 'Afghanistan?'

Pleasure didn't open his eyes. 'Six times,' he said.

'Wow! Going again?'

'Maybe,' Pleasure told him.

He could hear the slithery metallic sound of the tray being put down on the marble. He opened his eyes again and sat up with the masseur's help. His side felt a little less stiff. The pain was still there and his head ached. He took his glass of tea.

'Which way are you going?' he asked.

The Canadian grinned. 'Kabul.'

'Driving?'

'Right – we've got a VW camper,' the Canadian told him. 'There's two of us. I'm Uri.' He grinned. 'Ukrainian. And that's Jesse.' He pointed over at his companion who lay asleep. 'You got transport?'

Pleasure shook his head, which was a mistake. Pain stabbed at the back of his eyes and his vision blurred with blue tadpoles swimming across his retinas.

'You drive the other times?' Uri asked.

'Right,' Pleasure told him. He finished his tea. Lay back down again.

'Listen, I'm sorry,' he said. 'But I have to sleep.'

But now the masseur wouldn't leave him alone. Helping him to his feet, the Turk led him over to the step under one of the clam-shell fountains. Pleasure sat down and waited.

The Turk produced a large bowl of liquid soap and a wad of coarse sisal tow. Mixing a thick lather in the bowl, he scrubbed Pleasure from head to foot, dried him, wrapped him in two big towels, and led him back upstairs to his changing-room. There he dressed the American's scalp and bound his ribs with wide tape. Wrapping Pleasure in a sheet and two blankets, the Turk turned off the light.

It was the mullah's call to prayer that woke Pleasure. His head ached and his mouth felt and tasted like an abandoned ashtray. He fumbled for the light switch without any immediate memory of where he was. He looked at his watch. The naked band of white skin reminded him. Gingerly he swung his feet to the floor. The bandaging tugged at his ribs. He was stiff and his side hurt. His clothes were not in the room. He wrapped a towel round his waist and draped a blanket over his shoulders before going downstairs. Grey light seeped in through the dusty windows of the lobby. The clock above the reception desk showed him it was twenty past six. He rang the bell three times before the attendant came – the same fat Turk who had dressed his wounds.

Surprised to see Pleasure up so early, the masseur shook his head with disapproval as he shuffled sleepily over to examine Pleasure's skull. Satisfied with his inspection, he called the tea boy, gave him instructions, then opened the drawer in the desk. He had a message for Pleasure from the two Canadians.

Seeing that you've made the trip East so many times and know the road – how about coming along with us? FREE! You pay your food but nothing for the gas. This is if you want to go East again. We'd dig having you as a guide. Our VW is new and we've got great sounds. If you'd dig to come we're at the Aya Sofya Hotel, room 8. We'd like to pull out today.

Uri

Pleasure read the note through twice. He had two hundred dollars left and nothing else to do. He knew he could get a job making cases in Kabul. There were bound to be any amount of heavies organizing all sorts of insane numbers out of Afghanistan. A good case-maker could always make enough bread to get his own trip back together.

He wondered if half past six was too early to call. He decided it wasn't. The masseur found the number of their hotel for him. By the time he'd got through and told them he'd be over by nine, the boy was back with his clothes. They were clean and pressed. Now all he had to do was collect his new passport and his money from the restaurant and he was on his way.

CHAPTER THREE

Patrick Nolan sat at the ground-floor cocktail bar in the Intercontinental Hotel, Kabul. The time was three minutes to twelve o'clock noon, and this was his sixth day in the capital of Afghanistan. Tracing Goldberg into and out of Turkey had been simple. Apart from a fruitless stroll through the Blue Mosque district, all he had done was have the American's photograph copied. The Turkish narcotics squad had achieved the rest.

Afghanistan was not so easy. Initially he had contacted the police and offered them a reward for information. He had also left a photograph of Goldberg with a clerk at the mail desk in the central post office. Only with these actions already completed had he begun to recognize the problems. Hashish and opium were this country's major exports, therefore, though bribery was endemic, there was no guarantee whose bribe the local police and frontier guards would honour if they knew he belonged to the Department of Justice and that Goldberg was a dealer. The answer would probably depend on who paid last rather than on how much he paid ... meanwhile waiting for Goldberg was a drag, Patrick admitted, as he sipped gently at his fourth large Scotch. Excluded by his assignment from contacting the Embassy staff and being too shy to collect casual acquaintances, he found himself stranded on his own resources. The museum had been good for two mornings. The zoo was a disaster. Now there was nothing left that he wanted to see in the city and nowhere he wanted to be. He did not quite hate Kabul, but he was getting there fast.

His one fear was that the owners of the blue VW camper would have an accident in Iran. With Goldberg dead or hospitalized, he would either have to remain here in Kabul till his quarry recovered or – if Goldberg were killed – return home. Home being Frankfurt, he supposed. He beckoned the barman to refill his glass. The only other home he possessed made even Kabul seem friendly.

Patrick had not been home in the family sense since he'd left college. No, that was not quite true. He'd stopped by on his way to Vietnam. His longshoreman father had been predictably both drunk and violent – had called Patrick a fag without reason except that Patrick had spent five years at Cornell (though this was ample evidence of homosexuality in his father's eyes) – and his mother had wept, this also as usual. The only one of his six elder brothers present had been Ed the humourist – not that Patrick had been amused. Convinced he was on his way to Vietnam to be killed, he had expected to be taken seriously. He had said nothing but had not been back. Now he wrote the obligatory letters – Christmas, Easter and his mother's birthday – this was all. Which left him stuck with Frankfurt, he admitted now. Carrying his whisky out on to the terrace, he strolled down the steps to the pool.

Finding himself an isolated sun bed in one corner of the pool enclosure, Patrick put his glass down carefully on the lawn, took off his jacket, lay down and loosened his tie. From behind the dark glasses he'd put on when leaving the bar, he inspected and catalogued the crowd.

There were half a dozen rich Afghanis not pleased to be into their thirties – each with a Western girl friend. Two of them were into competitive muscle-flexing. *The Pool Club Gang.* Over to his right sat two families of Swedes on a United Nations advisory mission who were too bigoted, rather than too neutral, to use the American Club. Three jet-age commercial travellers stood by the outdoor bar. The rest were dope dealers . . . eight young American males with eleven chicks.

Presumably the dealers all knew each other but they lay in three separate groups. A case of the stags guarding their hinds, Patrick mused as he watched them. He knew they were dealers by their cameras (three Hasselblads, two Nikon Fs) and because they were not junkies. There could be no other reason for them to be in Kabul this late in the year. Five of the men he placed as New York Jewish and he would have taken any bets that at least two of them had been to school at Erasmus Hall — maybe three. Two of the girls had recently been on junk. Patrick could tell by their skins. No one had taught him this skill; he'd been in Vietnam when he'd found he possessed it. For three months he'd been a computer with its own particular binary code: junkie — non-junkie, junkie — non-junkie. Then he'd learnt how to switch himself off. He was never wrong. He knew it was not really the skin, but it was their skins he looked at — arms, neck, cheeks. At the most these two girls had been clean for a week. The boys were readying them for a smuggling run, he guessed. And no Goldberg.

Taking a quick sip at his glass, Patrick lay back again. The long concrete-and-glass curve of the Intercontinental reared over the pool as if about to devour the poolside guests. Occupying the crest of a low hill, the American hotel was the biggest building in town; also the most noticeable and the most opulent. Not more than one in a thousand of the local inhabitants could afford a cup of coffee at the prices charged. Not a good way to make friends, Patrick mused, rolling over to look down at the dusty capital. One more country ripe for revolution. He wished he'd obeyed his first instincts and followed his quarry overland instead of mundanely flying Iran Air. The dealers had the fun: that was rule one, he decided as he turned back to watch a tall, bronzed stag wrestle a blonde hind to the pool edge.

The dealer overbalanced. As he fell backwards into the water his right foot shot up to catch momentarily on the underlip of the blonde girl's blue bikini top. Patrick saw her bare breast . . . and, looking up, she saw that he saw and she smiled. He tried to answer. But was too late. The contact broke and he was left lying alone in the autumn sunshine.

The drive east from Istanbul took them six days. Kandahar was their goal. Here, in payment for his ride, Pleasure had promised to help the Canadians score twenty kilos of Afghani hashish – the hash that was to pay for their trip and earn them the capital to open a restuarant back home in Montreal. If they got it home. But that was their problem.

They had left Istanbul at ten o'clock in the morning – a bitter autumn morning with rain squalls whipping down off the moorland hills beyond the Sea of Marmara. Then, after six and a half hours, Ankara. The capital came heralded by mile after mile of country stripped bare of any vegetation capable of feeding a winter fire. Miles of unpainted clay shacks. Miles of the same numb-faced inhabitants plodding home in their dark suits, thick scarves, rubber overshoes and floppy caps.

Alphabet and clothes Westernized by government edict, smooth avenues in the city centre, skyscrapers, plate glass, jewels, Mercedes, Cadillacs ... Ankara a twentieth-century mini-America flaunting itself in the midst of Tsarist Russia and the threatening violence clamped down by the rain and the cloud and the cold and the ever-present uniforms backed by rifles and pistols and sub-machine-guns ... stubborn anger glimpsed in the shadows of a peaked cap as the Volkswagen swept past a bus stop – anger, bitterness, hate – but above all, stubbornness: stubborn waiting for eruption. Revenge on the leaders. Revenge for the years of betrayal. V O T E F O R M E S O T H A T I C A N B E M O R E I M P O R T A N T T H A N Y O U!

'Jesus! Let's get the hell out of this country,' Jesse, the younger of the two Canadians, had shouted above the beat of Janis Joplin, and they had driven on through the evening and through the night towards the Black Sea and Trabzon.

Driving was a nightmare. Livestock and their owners wandered at will on to the road. Trucks thundered down the crown; stopped where and when the drivers desired; overtook each other on the brow of hills.

Nine hundred and sixty kilometres to Trabzon. Pleasure at the wheel, they turned right before the tunnel under the basilica and drove uphill into the square where they breakfasted on grilled Black Sea *cipura,* flat loaves of white bread, coffee, and yoghurt solid as cream cheese.

Now the mountains, and they wound up through mist-flowing ravines and along the side of deep gorges with shrunken wind-warped pines writhing up the cliff face beneath blizzard clouds of thick, wet, grey wool. Dripping villages huddled for protection against the flank of the mountains; villages lapped by low waves of rotting refuse; mud hovels with roofs beaten from empty kerosene cans; kids throwing stones; giant sheep-dogs snapping and snarling as they chased the VW; glowering elders gobbing vicious jets of tobacco juice; still resplendent in Union Jack livery, the crumpled wreck of a Bedford camper glimpsed abandoned in a river-bed with a big white peace symbol painted on its roof – the end of one trip East.

At six thousand six hundred feet they ran into drifting snow across the plateau of Zigana Pass. Sun burst through the clouds and they stopped to crap on the white road edge with yellow patterns melting the snow as they peed and no one in sight so they could suddenly laugh and throw snowballs and leap and caper with the stiffness ebbing out of their limbs.

Now over moorland they swept down towards Erzurum and on to Horasan, where they swung right off the main road which led on to Russian Georgia. They drove two hours each, the last driver resting on the bed in the back. They had no trouble at the Iran border and were through and into Maku by eleven o'clock that night. After thirty-six hours on the road they were ready for luxury – hot baths at the Maku Motor Inn, dinner, *cuba libres* mixed from a bottle of Bacardi Uri had bought all the way back in Athens.

They awoke to sunshine. A wide, well surfaced road led them down the floor of a spreading valley between pleated hills bare of vegetation; skeletal hills with sandy-pale spines, brown ribs and deep trenches of mauve shadow. They passed neat villages of baked clay. Straw stacked on their roofs, the small houses glowed amber in the bright morning light; walled orchards with beehive watch-towers; pigeons floating overhead against a sun-bleached sky; plodding camels, their heads snake-swaying

54

on long necks; veiled women in long dresses sprinkled with blue flowers – blue against the evil eye – and smiling men, laughing children, no one throwing stones, no hate, no litter-washed squalor.

The burden of Turkey behind them, they drove slowly and lay in the sun for an hour after picnicking on fresh bread, sardines and ripe red apples. In the late afternoon they reached Tabriz. Then a long day to Teheran with the first part of the drive through the same burnt hills then across flat dull country.

They rested a day, obtained visas for Afghanistan, serviced the VW. More mountains, a night camped by the roadside and finally the border. Then Kandahar. The American at the wheel, they threaded their way through narrow streets crowded with gaily painted pony-traps, garish motor coaches and laden camels.

The houses were small, two-storied and whitewashed. Every doorway was a shop. Walls, windows, the doors themselves, all were draped with embroidery: waistcoats, shirt- and dress-fronts, bags, fur coats, desert carpets in dark earth shades, shelves laden with bubbly blue glass from Herat.

Side-streets rang with the hammering of metal-workers. They passed the street of the charcoal-burners, a black street of cavelike huts and coal-smudged men; the tanning district with its stink of urine and the gutters running thick with dye. Then the centre.

The moment their feet touched the pavement they were surrounded by a fighting mob of hustlers. Hands clawed at them as the Afghanis screamed the town's main product . . .

Hashish! Hashish! You want buy hashish, man? How much you want?

'*Jesus!*' Jesse gasped as they made it into the protection of the hotel doorway. 'Is this for real?'

'They have a one-crop economy,' Pleasure answered. Laughing, he led the way upstairs to find the owner and a room.

Feet up on their beds, they waited barely half an hour before there came a soft knock on the door.

'Mister Pleasure?' a voice whispered hoarsely.

The door creaked open just enough to allow a plump-cheeked Afghani to peep round inquiringly. Suspicious of his welcome, he smiled doubtfully. His clothes were Western, his teeth gold, his nose snub, his whole image obsequious.

'Enter Abdul,' Pleasure announced. 'Abdul the magic rip-off artist.'

'Not true,' Abdul protested as he sidled into their room. He closed the door with elaborate care – a clown conspirator. 'Not true,' he repeated.

He stood bowing and smiling while his hands anxiously washed each other, his whole body writhing with embarrassment. A gold-toothed, brown-skinned Labrador puppy, Pleasure thought.

'Then where's my twenty dollars?' he demanded.

'My father,' Abdul protested. 'Not letting me *out of house,* Mister Pleasure. Honest truth – I *swear* on Koran!'

'I gave him twenty for a half-kilo pair of shoes,' the American explained to the others. 'Never saw him again. How old are you, Abdul? Forty? And your father locks you up?'

The Afghani giggled. 'You see my father,' he assured them. 'Then you understand.'

'So where's the twenty?'

'You tell me buy shoes,' Abdul complained.

'So where's the shoes?'

'I sell.'

'So where's the money, then?'

Abdul flung up his arms in protest. 'Is now *two years,* Mister Pleasure. I am human not miracle man.'

'So the money's spent?'

Abdul nodded dolefully. 'Gone,' he admitted. 'All gone.'

'How long did you hold it?' the American asked.

'Eighteen months,' Abdul answered instantly. Then he saw their disbelief. 'One year?' he suggested hopefully. 'Six months?' He looked round anxiously. There was still no reassurance. He collapsed.

56

'Two weeks, Mister Pleasure,' he insisted. 'I swear to you — two weeks minimum!'

The Westerners laughed.

'And how's business now?' Pleasure asked.

Abdul shrugged. 'Difficult,' he explained. 'There is a new man at the American Embassy. You pay — he pays.'

'And he pays more,' Pleasure suggested.

The Afghani nodded dolefully. 'This man make too much trouble. Too many spy,' he explained. 'But for you, Mister Pleasure . . . '

'For me, Abdul?'

'Everything,' the Afghani promised.

'Can we score twenty safely, Abdul?' the American asked. 'Tonight?'

Abdul nodded. He held up both hands. 'Ten o'clock,' he told them. 'We meet same place like before.'

'Car?' Pleasure wanted to know.

Abdul nodded again.

They parked the bus in the shadows off the road. Abdul led them down a lane and into a small tea-house. Lit by a paraffin lamp, it was one room no more than three by four metres. Half a dozen Afghani men squatted barefoot on the carpet-covered platforms which ran round all but the entrance wall. By the door a small boy boiled water for tea on a charcoal brazier set on a stone. Underneath the platforms ran a shelf for shoes.

Other than a brief nod of greeting, the Afghanis ignored their entrance. Shedding their sandals, they clambered up on to the carpet. Abdul had chosen a corner. Looking at the American, he raised his eyes to the ceiling. Pleasure glanced up to see a wooden trap-door with a crack of light showing between the planks. Abdul winked, then called to the boy for tea.

The pot came served with a dish of sweet pink candies. There was no sugar. Pleasure explained to the two Canadians the Afghani trick of holding a sweet on the tongue then sucking the hot tea over it. The candies left a flavour in the mouth of mint and cheap scent.

Two men came in. Throwing their cowls back with a flick of their heads, they nodded to Abdul. Pleasure noticed they kept the open doorway covered with their bodies. Standing up, Abdul knocked twice on the trap door. It opened. Down came a wooden ladder.

'Quick!' Abdul ordered.

Up they climbed. Four of the Afghanis followed. There were already six men in the room which was the same size as the one below but lower ceilinged. The only light came from a charcoal fire laid on a clay trough set in the centre of the floor. At the head of the ladder a tall figure greeted them quickly, then passed them back to the end of the room. The light was so dim they could only see shapes at first; no details. The scent of the room was hashish. The walls, once whitewashed, were now smoked brown: the ceiling black. Backs against the walls, the Afghanis squatted, waiting and watching the foreigners. With their beaked noses and their shoulders hunched up over their knees, they resembled perched vultures. Their leader who had greeted them at the trap-door now sat between Pleasure and the two Canadians.

'Suleman,' he introduced himself.

He held out his hand. Pleasure took it. Hands firmly clasped, they inspected each other. Beardless, the Afghani looked to be in his early thirties. His face was both harder and more open than the usual Kandahar hustler. He could be cop or robber, Pleasure considered – but not an in-between-type Judas.

'You have pollen?' he asked.

Suleman nodded. 'First quality.'

'Yes?'

A large plastic bag materialized out of the shadows. Suleman opened it. Dug in his hand. Palm extended, he offered a small heap of golden brown powder for inspection.

The American took a pinch between thumb and first finger. Sniffed it. Spread it lightly to feel for stalk or earth, then kneaded it hard to test for the tackiness of resin. The scent was fresh and strong. He could feel no impurities and the resin

58

count was high. Satisfied, he passed what was now a crumbly ball to Jesse.

'It's good,' he told the Canadians.

Jesse rolled the ball a couple of times between his fingers, sniffed it, then passed it to Uri.

'How much?' Pleasure asked.

'Powder?'

'Pressed.'

Suleman shrugged. 'First we smoke,' he told them.

He flung the bag down the room to the old man squatting closest to the fire. This was Hassan, the factory's chief presser. He took a tablespoon of pollen in the palm of his left hand. Spat into it. Then he started to knead, using the heel of his right hand. He worked the powder into a flat fish shape then dropped it on to the charcoal for the resin to melt. Retrieving the piece, he added more pollen and more spit. Again he kneaded it with the heel of his right hand but also now he alternated this style with a squeezing movement in which he sandwiched the fish between the heel of his left hand and the first two fingers of his right, then clamped his left hand tightly closed. More heat. More pollen. More spit. He worked the fish each time till all the pollen and spit were absorbed into the whole. The rest of the men watched in silence. The atmosphere of the room was almost religious in its intensity. They watched a master at work.

Sitting exposed downstairs, Pleasure had felt a slight paranoia. Here, in the almost dark, that feeling had gone. Like the Afghanis, be squatted with his back resting against the wall. He was at home. This had been his life for ten years. Watching Hassan press, he felt no remorse — only a quiet sadness that his time was running out.

Perhaps he should have made enough to retire on when the game had still been easy. He could have, he knew, but he'd never tried to make big money. Had never done more than enjoy what he was doing while earning enough to support his own way of life; a way of life which had never been opulent or ostentatious, based as it was on his studio apartment in Ibiza at

59

forty dollars a month. No Ferrari, no Cadillacs, no night-clubs, no fancy restaurants – his only real conceit had been the kilo jars of pure Rosemary honey he'd stored on top of the ice box in the dairy; honey to eat with his breakfast yoghurt . . . and his Bultaco with the bored-out engine.

Smuggling had been a game – now it was a profession. If he'd wanted a profession he could have stayed home with his father in New York. And there wasn't much to choose between his father and half the young kids now in the dope business – despite their long hair. The kids were merely capable of greater self-delusion or hypocrisy. Both sides wanted to end up millionaires. At least his father admitted this. The heads pretended to be anti-materialistic revolutionaries, while they bought themselves ranches in Hawaii or Laguna Beach – the Brotherhood.

He had a feeling that it had been LSD that had brought the big-money concept into the business. It took capital to set up an acid laboratory, capital to buy the chemicals and pay the chemists. The profits had been enormous. All the greedy beady-eyed fraternity had come flocking in like vultures to the kill. Then, when the bottom had fallen out of the acid market, they'd moved on into the hashish business. Long-haired gangsters with guns playing at being spiritually enlightened. At least the Brotherhood had never sold bad acid, which was more than could be said for most of the other organizations.

Mini Mafias, Pleasure thought bitterly. If the acid came out bad from the test tube then don't waste it – add a little speed – a little strychnine; anything to give it a kick, and screw the casualties.

He was brought out of this reverie by Suleman nudging his side. He looked round. The factory owner held extended an open tobacco tin of red powder. The American thanked him. Taking the tin he spooned a small quantity on to the lid and flicked it into his mouth where he held it under his tongue. Then he passed the can to Jesse, who looked at him questioningly.

'Green tobacco ground with red chilli and hash pollen,' he

told the Canadian. 'It's hot,' he warned. 'And don't swallow or you'll lose your dinner.'

Jesse looked slightly sick. 'Do I have to?' he asked.

'Depends on whether you mind hurting their feelings.'

Jesse looked sicker.

'Take a little,' Pleasure told him. 'Smile and pass it on.'

Looking down the room he saw Hassan was finally satisfied with the press he'd achieved. Shuffling back against the wall, the old man passed the fish to the Afghani on his right who sniffed at it appreciatively, flicked at it with his index finger a couple of times to hear its ring, then bent it backwards and forwards.

'The bending's to check the resin is properly worked,' Pleasure explained. 'A bad press will break or crumble. So will hash with a low resin content.'

The fish went round the room. In turn each man made the same critical inspection. Again there was a feeling of taking part in a religious ritual. Finally Suleman handed the fish to the American.

Weighing around thirty grams, the piece was warm, smooth and flexible. He held it up to his ear. Flicked it. A dead sound would have indicated an incomplete press. This rang hard. Its scent was thick. Its colour was burnt honey. He handed it to Jesse.

'Feel it,' he told him. 'It's good shit, well pressed and strong enough to pin your ears back.'

Which was true, as he soon found out.

Suleman prepared the water pipe himself. The water container was a one-foot high, blue-and-white glazed pottery vase. Into this fitted the clay bowl with its stem wrapped in damp cloth to seal the joint. The mouthpiece was a long bamboo which stuck up nearly vertically from the side of the vase. The bottom of the pipe bowl was protected by fine copper mesh.

On to this Suleman placed half a dozen glowing shards of charcoal from the fire. Then he broke the fish into fragments which he laid over the coals.

61

As reward for his pressing, Hassan was given the honour of lighting the pipe. His two neighbours held flaming matches over the hashish. Standing up to the mouthpiece, Hassan took two deep breaths of air, then, emptying his lungs completely, he put his lips to the bamboo. He drew the smoke in short drags, held it for a moment, then exhaled in a burst of rapid-fire coughs which were deliberate – intended to force smoke and oxygen up into the brain.

The pipe travelled to the right. As each man smoked the room became more totally fume-bound. The solemn silence was over. Hassan broke into a long rambling story. Pleasure caught only a few words but these were enough to get the gist. It was a peasant farmer's tale of how good the crops had been long, long ago. Here the crop was hashish, in Ibiza it would have been almonds or *algaroba* beans. Grapes in Provence, corn in the Midwest; the story was always the same: it was the springboard to old men's memories.

The pipe came to Suleman. Silence. His left-hand neighbour lifted the bowl free of the vase to allow the factory owner to clear the stale smoke from the water vessel. He stood with his left foot raised on the fire-brick. He blew three clear trumpet notes through the bamboo. Every face was turned to him. He nodded. His neighbour clamped the bowl down tight. His shoulders came back square to open his lungs. Then he dragged. He dragged with incredible speed and strength. Sparks flew from the charcoal. Flames leapt. Leapt halfway to the ceiling. Red neon lit and re-lit the room. In minutest detail the faces of the watching Afghanis jumped into focus. Vanished. Re-appeared. Vanished. This was no challenge – it was total victory.

'Jesus!' Jesse whispered.

Pleasure stood up. Now it was up to him. He knew the Canadians would not smoke. They wanted to keep their heads clear for bargaining. He understood their attitude. It wasn't his. Never had been. The pipe was as intrinsic a part of Afghan tradition as the hand pressing. This was the romance: travelling three thousand miles to sit at night surrounded by cloaked tribesmen in a small smoky room in Kandahar or Mazar-i-Sharif.

Here this pipe was equivalent to the Spanish *macho:* the masculinity test of a primitive male society. If you passed, the Afghanis were your friends for ever. If you failed, you were too unimportant even to be mocked. To come this far and then not enter into their way of life seemed not only idiotic to Pleasure but also to deny the romance. And without the romance you were just one more Western businessman plundering the East for profit.

Here was his test. He smiled, first to himself, then to the watching tribesmen. He didn't try for a bugle note. Failure would have been too silly. One flame was his ambition, and then to get out of the room on his own two feet. He emptied his lungs as Hassan had done – squeezed them empty and slowly inhaled, on and on with his eyes on the bowl. Almost at the end of that inhalation he saw the first spark jump. He hit instantly and fast. *Drag Drag Drag In – Out In – Out In – Out.* The heat of the smoke seared his lungs. There were tears in his eyes. He knew he had to fall or stop. But the flames caught. The room leapt into light. Faces opened to him: smiling faces that egged him on. He hit twice more. Crazy conceit, he knew, even as he dragged, but the flames danced and the Afghanis clapped. He had to. Then he was through. He smiled again and sank back on to his heels, shoulders against the wall.

'Still alive?' Jesse asked.

Pleasure waved the question aside. He was far too involved with waiting to talk. Then the hash struck. It came in on him in rolling waves that cast him back against the wall. He could feel his head being pushed deep into the clay brick – so deep that his ears were spread from his head like pinned-out butterfly wings. That was his body's feeling. His mind was clear. He felt everyone in the room watching him. This was the familiar paranoia of an overdose – something he'd long ago learnt to deal with.

There is nothing to fear, he whispered to himself – nothing to fear but fear itself. What was the worst that could happen?

He could pass out. He could vomit. Neither mattered. The Afghanis might laugh at him. He let this picture drift on to the screen. He lay on the floor with his head lolling over a pool of sick. The Afghanis were standing. They were pointing at him. Laughing at him. Laughing and laughing. He started to laugh at himself. He looked so totally ridiculous lying there. Casualty of pride.

The screen cleared. The Afghanis *were* laughing. And he was laughing. Suleman had the pipe again. Flames danced and danced till finally the factory owner's lungs erupted.

'Easy,' he cautioned as he swung the mouthpiece to the American. 'Easy.'

The flames had leapt as high as his face and only now, a minute later, could he get his lungs back together so he could speak – and then only one word. Easy! Before he was off coughing again; coughing and crying and smiling all at the same time and his teeth so white, his whole face softening as Pleasure watched, losing its businessman's keenness, losing everything but laughter. Both of them laughing and laughing.

'Eee ... ' he went.

'Eee ... '

And they slapped their right hands hard together with joy of sharing this moment. Total mirth – nothing held back.

Something dragged at Pleasure's sleeve. He turned. Uri leant across his partner.

'How much?' he wanted to know. His voice seemed petulant. The ignored outsider.

What a crazy question, Pleasure thought. *How much for heaven?*

He shrugged helplessly as renewed laughter hit him. Hit him so hard his solar plexus ached with strain.

'Ask him,' he gasped. 'It's your shit.'

CHAPTER FOUR

The Kabul river divides the capital of Afghanistan into two main sections. The right bank is modern Kabul. The men wear suits, ties and well polished pointed shoes (Italian design *circa* 1950). Unveiled young women teeter on high heels and smile publicly as they strut their asses. Here are the government offices, embassies, the Royal Palace and concrete apartment buildings. The streets are tarred and shaded by acacias. There are three fountains, four cinemas, four mosques, and more than a dozen pharmacies: *Junk City* – the pharmacies are the tourist draw. And there are streets of small hotels where the travellers stay: Westerners – the heads, the freaks, the addicts.

Crossing to the left bank his first day in the capital, Pleasure had an impression of traversing a frontier far more real than any of the national borders on the road east from Istanbul. This side of the river all the glass and concrete trappings of modern Kabul were a forgotten illusion. Dress was traditional. The women were robed and fully veiled. The men wore headcloths, loose shirts, embroidered waistcoats and baggy cotton pants bunched up into their groins.

The pavement was a marketplace. Shaving their customers, barbers squatted underfoot in apparent indifference to the passing crowd. The lee of every wall angle served as a restaurant. Pots of chicken and mutton stew bubbled on charcoal braziers. Brass trays of boiled rice sat in the dust beside piles of unleavened bread. You could eat for five cents and die of amoebic dysentery even before hepatitis killed you. Flies were everywhere: house flies, fruit flies, horse flies, camel flies. Laden camels plodded after their owners. Donkeys tripped by on high heels with the water-cans carried on their wooden

saddles splashing dark patches on to the grey dust of the streets
– a maze of streets: narrow streets of low houses out of which
spilled all the noise and bustle of the market; streets containing
every kind of artisan: basket-weavers, metal-workers,
carpenters, mat-plaiters, leather-workers, tailors, embroiderers;
streets of vegetable stalls and fruit stalls; butchers,
yoghurt-sellers, tool merchants, grain merchants.

The American turned right the other side of the bridge. The
river was almost dry after the long summer and the stench of
six months' accumulated defecation choked him as he hurried
on past the rug venders squatting like perched vultures on the
parapet.

Struggling through the throng of pleading commission men,
he entered the money market. Two floors of dark booths faced
inward on to a courtyard. The American climbed the stairway
and walked quickly down the balcony to a stall in the far
corner.

An old henna-bearded Afghani sat cross-legged on the carpet
beside a Chubb safe which had to be valuable if only as an
antique. Leaving his shoes by the door, the American took the
papery hand the old man offered him.

'Salaam Aleikum,' he murmured as he squatted down,
'Salaam Hadji. Khob-asti?'

Gravely the Afghani returned his salutations. Then clapped.
A boy came. Saw the American. Nodded. Left.

Five minutes later the Hadji's plump, middle-aged banker
son came hurrying in. He smiled on seeing the American.

'So,' he asked as he sank down beside him. 'Back in business?
I had bad news of you.'

Pleasure laughed. Financier and fixer to the trade, Mahomed
had an intelligence network which ringed the world.

'Two years?' the Afghani asked.

'Nineteen months.'

'Bad?'

'What's bad?' The American shrugged. 'I'm alive. How are
things here?'

'Difficult,' Mahomed admitted. 'Your embassy demands

arrests. We give them arrests.' He waved in the direction of his safe. 'What would you?' he asked. 'We need foreign aid. Smoke?'

The American took a cigarette. 'How difficult?' he asked.

'We give them the small fish,' Mahomed told him. 'Five kilos, ten kilos. Here,' he flicked a gold Dunhill – watched the American inhale. 'What else can we do?' he asked.

'But the trucks get through?'

Mahomed nodded. 'Trucks ... planes.' He drew on his cigarette. 'And you?' he asked.

Pleasure sat studying his cigarette end. Finally he shrugged. 'I'm broke,' he admitted. Then he looked straight at the banker, who sat purse-lipped watching him.

'I need to make a run,' he said.

Slowly Mahomed nodded. 'Big?' he asked.

'Big.' Pleasure spoke hardly above a whisper. 'The Big One, Mahomed. The one you always talked about.'

For a moment a smile touched the Afghani's lips – only for a moment. Then he looked away from the American, at the safe, then at his father, and then at the open doorway. His fingers played gently through a string of amber worry-beads.

'How many kilos?' he asked.

'One hundred,' Pleasure told him. 'I need three thousand dollars for the hashish, two thousand for a truck and say five for expenses.'

'Ten thousand?'

'Ten thousand,' Pleasure agreed. 'You front ten grand and we net seventy thousand each if I wholesale it in the States.'

The banker nodded slowly. 'The Hundred Kilo Club,' he murmured. Click click went the beads. Then he looked up. His eyes were almost sad.

'How many times did I tell you?' he asked. 'Do the Big One, I told you. Do it while it's easy.' He shrugged. 'And now you come.' His beads dropped. His hands rose. Spread palms up – plump pads of pale chocolate.

'You're being followed,' he said. Then suddenly his voice was wheedling and his eyes were huckster's eyes.

'Friendship?' he pleaded. 'Would it be friendship to see you jailed?' His eyes darted to the doorway. He clapped. The boy came. He ordered coffee. Turned back to the American.

'All those years when it was easy . . . why did you wait?' he asked.

Pleasure shrugged. He felt older. Tired. 'You're sure?'

'That you're being followed?' Mahomed nodded. 'An American. He's been here a week.'

For a moment they looked at each other . . . but this time it was the American who looked away. At the doorway. At the sunlight bright on the corrugated tin roof of the block across the courtyard.

'And if I kick my tail?' he asked. 'Kick him for good?'

It was ten o'clock the following morning when Patrick finally spotted his quarry. The narcotics agent sat drinking tea on the balcony of a first-floor restaurant in the centre of modern Kabul. He'd been there for an hour. From where he sat he could watch Aziz Stores (the only shop in town to stock real American peanut butter), the Softee Ice-cream Parlour, two pharmacies and, diagonally across the intersection, a bakery which baked genuine Brownies to a recipe taught the owner by one more nice Jewish girl on the run from Brooklyn Heights.

Goldberg, munching an apple, came strolling down Chicken Street towards the Stores. He smiled in between bites; smiles for everyone – and the smiles got answers from all sides. Patrick knew him at once. Not *recognized* – though that he did too – but knew him from school. There'd been a dozen Goldbergs he'd longed to emulate. That casual loose-limbed walk and the smiles.

He was easy to tail. Apparently indifferent to the stench of sour urine the Afghanis used for tanning, Goldberg window-shopped slowly up the street of fur stores before following the main avenue along past the State Bank with its sentries and rusty rifles towards the Khyber Restaurant; this last, a long, modern, single-storey cafeteria with plastic serve-yourself trays, stainless-steel slop bins, chrome, and that special cafeteria smell of soap, sour milk, friers and over-boiled stew.

Goldberg paused outside the Khyber to inspect the array of cars and campers for sale. Half the countries in Europe were represented by the licence plates plus five from the States and one from Canada. The owners sat passively waiting at the sunlit tables on the pavement. Long hairs were heading East. Shaven scalps and Hari Krishna topknots were either stuck right here on a pharmacy trip or on their way back West. Nodding a general greeting, Goldberg went on into the cafeteria where he sat half an hour over a cup of tea and a new *Time* magazine he bought at the cash desk. Then he went out, crossed the bridge, walked up past the money market and entered the central post office.

Patrick bought three picture postcards while he waited outside – one card of the market and two showing tribesmen of the Hindu Kush. One card could go to his mother. He had no destinations for the other two. Depressed by this thought, and already hot, sweaty and in need of a drink, he followed Goldberg back to the Khyber. Half an hour later his quarry again went outside, this time passing the Kabul Hotel to turn left by the Ariana Airline office.

For a moment Patrick had hopes that Goldberg might be on his way out of Afghanistan. No such luck. Ignoring the ticket office, Goldberg continued up the street to the coach park. Patrick watched him speak to a half dozen Afghanis then return to the Khyber where he collected a back-pack and a long thin aluminium tube. Ten minutes later he boarded a bus for Bamiyan. Patrick checked what time the first coach left the following morning. His quarry's pack had looked heavy and its contents had rung metallically as the driver had hauled it up on to the baggage rack.

Could it contain a radio, Patrick wondered, as he strolled back towards his hotel. Other than an aerial, he could think of nothing that would fit the tube. And a radio would make sense if they had a landing strip somewhere up in the hills.

Half an hour later, sitting slouched over his first Scotch of the day, he thought of a rifle barrel.

Pleasure was last off the bus at Bamiyan. There was no hurry. He had nothing to do but select his post and wait. There was still an hour till moonrise. The shops in the small marketplace were lit by pressure lamps. They smelt faintly of kerosene. There were only a dozen and they were stalls more than shops: stalls with ramps of fruit and vegetables sloping down to the road. The owners sat muffled up behind the ramps with, behind them, the sparsely stocked shelves: a packet of candles, matches, a can of cooking oil, half a dozen cooking pots, a roll of printed Russian cotton and a few plastic mugs. The evening was cold. There were few people abroad and those who were hurried by with their hands and faces hidden deep in their *chapans*.

The American bought red chillis, rice, onions, oranges and a kilo of leeks. Then he turned north out of town. The path climbed up out of the valley. In ten minutes he was clear of the houses. A further half hour and he'd left the trees behind. Now he clambered up the open rocky hillside. The cold did not bother him. There was no wind and the weight of his pack soon had him sweating.

He'd been climbing an hour when the moon rose. He stopped – first to watch, then to stay. This was as good a place as any. He found a sandy hollow. Unrolled his borrowed sleeping-bag, took off his boots and wriggled in.

There was something strongly sensuous in this total solitude: the warmth of the bag, the clear moon with its frost-promising halo, and the long shadows of the surrounding rocks. Hands interlocked between his thighs, he found himself squirming with delight. It was like being a small boy again. Summer camp. Canoe treks. Freedom from the responsibility of daily loving a doting mother and an over-ambitious father. Only by yourself could you safely play yourself – that had been the lesson of his youth. The rest of the time it was easier to play at being whatever it was that was demanded of you. Fools fought the system. The wise conformed as long as their sentence lasted.

70

Then they got out for good.

He lay flat on his back now, hands behind his head. Down below the tree-line an owl softly hooted and a dog barked in reply. Something rustled through the dry grass to his left: a mouse perhaps, or a mountain civet. Above him a meteor shot loose into oblivion. For a moment the arc of its passing lay on his retina. Then nothing. That was the danger . . .

Faces came out of the past: Dutch Pete, Rob the Black, Tony's Maria, Pepe the Catalan poet with the tough man guerilla moustache — he'd drowned himself at the end of the summer of '69. Red Francesca. Little Gerry who'd overdosed in Rome. Bad Alec, dead on his bike. Kissing Cousin Kate so pale and innocent wandering the whore streets of Barcelona with her mind blown to bits — a nice clean little rich girl from the Midwest, who took so many acid trips she finally never got back.

Junk. Speed. Too much acid. More and more, that's how it was getting to be. Heavy, Pleasure decided, and, sitting up, rolled himself a joint on which to get to sleep.

Pleasure woke at first light. He lay buried deep and warm in his bag. It was a cocoon, outside which the cold held the mountain silent. He held his breath as he listened: no bird, no animal — even the air was still and scentless.

As he sat up his bag crackled with his movement. There was frost on the ground and, a hundred yards below where he'd camped, the mountainside vanished into thick mist.

He decided coffee could wait for sun up. There was no point in making a fire. He'd be shivering cold long before he could collect sufficient twigs from beneath the scant scrub. Boots on, he shouldered his gear and climbed quickly towards the spur which plunged away to the east from the main body of the mountain. Beyond this was his goal.

It took him an hour to reach the crest. The ridge had become an outline against the rising sun so that he clambered into warmth with his head bowed to protect his eyes. Gold flickered off the flints and granite. The first bird flew: a brown-winged falcon circling lazily up to its sentry post. He paused briefly at the top, long enough to look back down to the breaking mist. No one followed.

He had intended to make coffee. Now he was only anxious to reach the next valley, the stream and the lake. Would the tea-house still be there? The tea-house with its two rooms for rent and its revolting food – the one place in all his travels where even he had contracted dysentery. He almost ran. His boots slithered on loose shale as he scrambled down the path.

The valley was narrow, the last tendrils of mist still trapped in the sweeping branches of the acacia trees growing along the lower slopes of the mountain. He jumped the first irrigation ditch. There was a narrow log bridge but he wanted to jump. Wanted to leap and prance and sing. He could see the meadow below. It was as he remembered it – a mile-wide carpet of thick juicy grass spread across the floor of the valley. The stream ran down the middle. On its near bank stood the tea-house. Clay walls, flat roof, it squatted on a scar of red trodden earth. Smoke leaked from the diamond vents in the chimney.

'Khob-asti?' he shouted as he burst out of the trees.

As long as the chef hadn't changed all would be well.

He hadn't. At a hundred yards Pleasure recognized the assassin. He was older – so were his clothes – and even more obese. He was still as dirty and still had the same growth of piebald beard sticking out at right angles from his chin and cheeks.

At the American's shout he'd eased his bulk out through the tea-house door. Now he saw his guest and knew him. Arms outflung in welcome he broke into a waddling trot.

Pleasure stopped short and swept him a low bow. It was the only immediate action he could think of that might avoid the horror of the coming embrace. It didn't. In a moment he was swept into the cook's encircling odour of years old garlic sweat. Even this short effort had Nazur panting. His whole body quivered with each breath.

'Khob-asti?' he demanded.

'Khob-asti.'

'Jor-asti?'

'Jor-asti?'

He dragged the American to the house. 'Chai?' the Afghani offered. 'Coffee?'

'I cannot,' Pleasure protested. He had rehearsed his explanation – learnt the words by heart.

'This is a pilgrimage,' he told the Afghani. 'I have come to be alone. I must eat only rice and what I find in the lake and the meadow, and I must cook it myself.'

'But where will you sleep?' Nazur protested.

The American pointed up the valley. 'By the lake.'

'Will you sit?' Nazur gestured to a rope bed set in the sun. The sight of it set his guest scratching in memory.

'It would be against my promise to Allah,' he explained. He saw the disappointment in Nazur's face. 'For five days I must be alone – then I will share your hospitality,' he reassured the Afghani. 'You are still alone?'

'Always alone,' Nazur sighed. 'What must be must be,' he murmured sadly. 'All is the will of Allah.'

Or too much food and two few baths, Pleasure thought as he took a deep breath before clasping the tragic figure to his breast.

'I remember you always,' he told Nazur. 'In my travels you accompany me – you and the image of this valley.'

Gratified, the Afhani smiled. 'Then go with Allah,' he said. 'And may he watch over you.'

CHAPTER FIVE

Pleasure had made camp at the head of the lake. Below him the valley flowed down like an emerald river between tree-fringed mountain banks of slate-grey shadow shot with sunlit sorrel. Beside where he sat the stream fell over a barrier of calcium-streaked rock into a small pool. Spray sprinkled the banks of the pool, the grass so lush the poppies, yellow cowslips and clover were almost strangled. A bed of wild mint scented the air.

The setting was so perfect that now, as he watched the distant figure climb towards him, he felt regret rather than relief that the waiting was over. Five days, he had told Nazur. It had taken only four – and at that he was surprised. For the last three days he had spotted surreptitious movement on the mountainside – movement accompanied by the occasional glint of sunlight on binoculars or telescope.

He had expected one meal of Nazur's cooking to suffice. Creeping close to the tea-house on the second night, he had checked that his tail was sleeping there. Which he was. So either his tail was a man of exceptional fortitude or he had a cast-iron gut. Either way, he was now defeated, Pleasure saw, as he watched the narcotics agent stop hurriedly to crouch behind a gorse bush, then stop again only a hundred yards closer to the lake.

He smiled as he watched the third hiding, this halt amongst the grey smooth boulders by the waterside. There was a definite stagger in the man's gait as he came on up the valley in the pale evening sunlight with the kingfishers flashing over the crystal water, a pair of hawks wheeling, finches whistling, a poised heron waiting, and dumb desperation in the way the agent bent forward into the calm slope of the path, his hands tight by his sides and his feet advancing, plod plod, stumble plod, up on over the uneven sward.

'Motherfucker,' Pleasure whispered exultantly.

He'd won. He sat there apparently serene. He held a borrowed fishing-rod in his left hand. In four days he had caught nothing. Hadn't really tried. This bait had probably been taken long ago. He didn't care. He had been satisfied to just hold the rod and watch the float below bob in the eddies of the pool.

'Suffer, motherfucker,' he whispered as the agent stumbled, searched desperately for cover like a hunted animal. Found none. Grabbed at his gut. Doubled over as the spasm hit him.

Patrick's groan drifted up the valley. He had lost all control. His bowels contracted. He stood there bowing to the evening sun, worshipping – the sulphur dribble on his thigh backs a sacrifice to a punitive puritan God.

He wanted to cry. He felt no hate for his supposed quarry who sat so superior up there on the flat rock above the waterfall pool, not even anger – just desolation. He wanted to stand there and weep till someone rescued him. Only he wasn't a child any more. Nor ever would be again.

That comfort had gone together with so many others: certitude, faith, direction. He shrugged.

'Shit,' he murmured to himself. His soiled trousers dragged as he walked and he managed to smile briefly at the appropriateness of his exclamation.

'Shit!' This time he said the word out loud. He'd reached the pool. He looked up. Their eyes met. His quarry sniffed, then nodded agreement.

'You stink ... and do you mind telling me what you're pretending to be?' he asked pointing at the heavy binoculars and the Nikon with telephoto lens which hung round Patrick's neck.

'I'm an ornithologist,' Patrick answered. He did not sound very convincing – not even to himself.

'Pretending to be,' his quarry corrected. 'We both know

what you are.'

Patrick surrendered. 'Then why the fuck don't you move?' he demanded.

He had not known what he was going to say and now, even as his legs crumpled under him, he had time for surprise at his own forthrightness. He sat supported by his left arm, one cheek of his ass on a stone. As he laid his camera and binoculars on the grass, he wondered if he would have strength or time to get up when the next spasm hit – not that it mattered, he thought. His trousers were already so disgusting that he might as well sit where he was and at least have the satisfaction of punishing Goldberg with his smell.

'Well?' he asked looking up again.

'Move? You mean from this rock?'

'Rock! From this whole goddam area. I'm dying,' Patrick told him.

'And that's my fault?'

'Whose else?' Patrick demanded. 'Fuck!' he added.

His hands cradled his stomach. The sky spun. Sweat poured down his face. Pure liquid spurted through the thin linen of his pants. Christ! he prayed. He staggered to his feet. Foot against foot, he forced off his shoes, dropped his trousers and clambered down into the stream. There he stood, the filth washing from his legs in brown driblets which stained the pool, and his pants held in bewildered disgust. The water was ice cold from the mountains.

'Why the hell did they have to let you escape?' he complained. 'Robert goddam Goldberg!'

'Pleasure,' Pleasure corrected him. Rod held under his thigh, he sat calmly rolling a second joint.

'Pleasure! Where, for God's sake?' Patrick plunged his pants into the water. 'Here?' he asked. 'You like it here?'

'It'll do,' Pleasure answered. He bent down, right hand proffering the joint. 'Smoke?'

'I don't.'

'You should,' Pleasure baited.

'Screw you!' Patrick snapped half-heartedly.

76

'You have the energy?' Pleasure asked.

Patrick smiled despite himself. Up this close there seemed no way for them to be enemies.

'Catch!' He flung his dripping pants up on to Pleasure's rock and climbed after them. Pleasure reached down a hand to help.

'They won't dry,' he told Patrick.

Patrick shrugged. Giving the bottom end of his pants to Pleasure to hold, he started to twist. A slight breeze stirred coldly round his wet legs. Sunset in an hour.

'I guess you're right,' he said. 'You really like it here?'

Their eyes met over the wrung-out pants. There had been pleading in Patrick's voice. 'Sure, it's beautiful but ... ' Shrugging again he gave up the effort to explain. He looked down at his legs. His knees stuck out from under his shirt-front. 'Maybe I'm prejudiced,' he suggested. He looked back up at his fellow American and they both laughed.

'I guess this isn't in the manual,' Patrick added.

Spreading out his trousers to dry, he sat down beside Pleasure. The stone warmed his ass. With his eyes, he followed the course of the stream, which flowed placidly on down the valley he had just so painfully ascended.

'Jesus! I must have looked a dope.'

The same age almost, they looked strangely alike. They were both over six feet, both dark-eyed and black-haired. Each had a beaked nose and a long chin. Patrick was heavier, his face sad, disappointed. The dysentery had flushed him out. A sense of the idiocy of their situation had been growing on him; there had never been any clear picture in his mind of what would occur if this meeting took place. Now it had.

Even with his pants on to support some remaining dignity, Patrick would still have been woefully ill prepared. Possibly the situation would have been easier if Goldberg – or Pleasure, the Irishman corrected himself – had turned out to be some sort of vicious freak. He wasn't. In fact there was this comfortable, though disconcerting, sense of kinship. Patrick doubted that this feeling was just New York City discovering New York City on a rock in the middle of the wilderness. He chuckled suddenly. Shaking his head in wonder more than bewilderment, he glanced over at Pleasure.

'I guess I've really fucked up,' he said.

'Looks that way,' Pleasure agreed. 'Sure you don't want to smoke?'

Patrick took the cigarette. Pleasure had used an American flag paper. Patrick looked at it a moment — the blue and white stripes, the one line of stars that still showed.

'Well, well . . . ' he murmured. 'Here we go — up in smoke.' He took a deep drag. 'You know something,' he said as he inhaled. 'This is the first joint I've had since Vietnam.'

'Hardly goes with the job.'

'True.'

A wood hoopoe flashed across the surface of the pool. He had dark wavy lines resembling writing on his wings and a long curved beak like a snipe.

'Kind of interesting to an ornithologist,' Pleasure remarked as they watched the bird swoop away into the trees to their left. 'Parts of Africa the natives believe if you eat that hoopoe alive you get the gift of tongues. Allah's written word on his wings or something.'

He reeled in his hook. 'Want coffee?'

'Sure.'

'Bring your pants. I'll fix a line.'

The embers still glowed in the stone fireplace Pleasure had built. Adding a few sticks, he blew up the flames.

Patrick watched him set the pan. 'Mind if I ask what you're doing here?' he asked.

'Waiting for you.'

Patrick nodded. 'That's what I finally figured,' he said. 'First off I thought you were expecting a plane.'

Whirling round, 'A plane!' Pleasure shrieked indignantly. 'Who in hell do you think I am? With you following me I can't even raise the bread for a half-shot truck.'

'What?' Patrick gasped.

'What goddam what?'

'You *can't* be broke.'

'There's a law against that too?' Pleasure demanded.

Aghast, Patrick squatted staring up at him.

'Then we're stuck here,' he protested. 'I mean ... Well, Jesus! You're meant to be some kind of a big-wheel gangster.'

'Me?'

'You,' Patrick told him. 'Bob Goldberg – alias Pleasure. Ha goddam ha! Joke. *And* dangerous. Shit!' he groaned, grabbing his gut.

Pleasure watched him dash for the trees. 'So who says I'm not dangerous?' he shouted. Then he hammered two sticks into the earth a metre back from the fire and strung up Patrick's pants.

'Bleeding?' he asked as the Irishman came hobbling back.

Patrick nodded. 'You plan this?'

'The dysentery? Kind of,' Pleasure admitted sheepishly.

'Mother!'

'How in hell else was I going to make us talk?' Pleasure asked. Digging into his pack, he pulled out a tube of Lomatil which he threw to the narcotics agent. 'Take one every four hours.'

'Strong?'

'The best,' he assured the Irishman. He watched him swallow a pill. 'Next thing you'll tell me you thought I had a gun.' He saw Patrick's embarrassed smile.

'You did!' he accused.

The Irishman nodded at the aluminium rod case. 'Ever see *The Day of the Jackal*?' he asked. 'The way the assassin carried his rifle?'

'Oh no ... !' Pleasure protested.

The sight of his indignant quarry sitting there shaking his head was too much. Despite the pain in his gut, Patrick began to laugh. 'You!' he gasped. 'I mean, *you* ... '

'Me what?' Pleasure demanded. 'So who's so hot? You, for Christ's sake?'

Tears running down his cheeks, all Patrick could do was wave weakly.

Laden with Patrick's possessions, the climb up from Nazur's

tea-house in the dark cleared Pleasure's head. He'd paid the Afghani an extra two dollars as compensation for depriving him of his guest. Panting, he lowered Patrick's heavy pack to the ground by their fire.

'What's in this?' he complained.

Patrick turned to grin proudly up at him. 'Bird books,' he said.

'For real?'

'Sure – look.' Patrick unstrapped his pack to display the nine fat reference volumes he'd acquired in Istanbul. He expected applause but Pleasure just smiled and slowly shook his head.

'You're nuts,' he said. 'Apart from it's nearly winter – ever see a birdwatcher without a tan?'

Deflated, Patrick turned back to the flames. He gave the embers a poke – which helped neither him nor the fire. 'You're not very polite,' he accused. 'What else could I come East as – a dealer?'

Pleasure grinned. Collecting water from the lake, he set a pan to boil for rice, before squatting down beside the Irishman.

'Cigarette?' he offered.

No response.

'Don't sulk,' Pleasure baited.

This time Patrick looked up. 'You shouldn't put me down,' he said. 'I mean – shit! All I am is a glorified clerk, right? And I found you. Is that so bad?'

'Bad?' Still smiling, Pleasure shrugged. 'Look,' he pointed out, 'I'm just the fox. Maybe you should ask your boss.' He fed three sticks in under the pan before chancing a glance at his companion. Their eyes met. Patrick managed a sheepish grin.

'What in hell got you into this?' Pleasure asked.

'Justice?' Patrick shrugged. He'd been in Vietnam – a clerk attached to the S.I.B. When the heroin plague hit they'd transferred him to Narcotics. Three months before his discharge the Bureau had a recruitment officer come by. O'Farrell. Patrick shrugged again.

'From then on it was ethnic loyalty,' he said. He smiled. 'You know how it is. The bread sounded good and what else was there? Back to school?' He gave the fire a prod.

'You dig going back to school after two years off?'

'How far had you got?' Pleasure asked.

'Two years into my Masters'.' Suddenly morose, he sat staring into the flames. His mother's dreams of his becoming a professor. Driving him with the threat of her tears. Eleventh-century German literature. Some career!

'Can you imagine?' he asked. 'All those kids scaring the shit out of you for the rest of your life.' He shuddered. 'Christ! I could do with a drink.'

'No booze till your stomach's straight,' Pleasure warned. 'We'll eat – then I'll roll a joint.' He poured rice into the boiling water. 'What got you to Vietnam?' he asked. 'You could have got a deferment.'

Patrick again looked sheepish. 'Sure,' he admitted. 'I guess it was the easiest way I could find of dropping out.' He looked at Pleasure. Smiled.

'You see, my family . . . the army's peace!'

'That bad?' Pleasure asked.

Patrick nodded. 'It's different for you,' he said. 'Being Jewish. Your family has bread.'

Pleasure raised an eyebrow. 'That a crack?'

Patrick shrugged. 'Have it – getting it – losing it. Bread's your thing, right? Hard-hat Irish, we think we've lucked it if we get some kind of status.' Suddenly thinking of Kennedy back in Istanbul. 'You ever see a Jew in the State Department?' he asked. 'See? For you people it's a lousy job.'

Pleasure smiled. 'Maybe,' he admitted.

'And your family do have bread.'

'That in my report?' Pleasure asked.

'Experience,' Patrick told him. 'Jewish kids on the road. Back home somewhere, they all have bread.' He smiled. 'Especially dope dealers. How else would you get bail?'

'Four lids of grass,' Pleasure protested. 'The bail wasn't that high.'

'Is that all?' Patrick looked surprised. 'And you skipped?'

Pleasure nodded. He'd been in his third year at Yale – the

draft threatening – and then his father's dress factory. He'd been bored by his studies. He hated the rag trade and he thought the war insane. Nor had he ever been close to his father. His arrest had been the catalyst. He'd bailed himself out with two thousand dollars of the sixty-two hundred and forty-eight he'd inherited from his maternal grandmother. Quitting school had taken three days and he'd wasted one more day in attempting to explain to his parents why he abjured the clothing industry. He'd already bought a one-way ticket to Marrakesh.

'On six thousand goddam dollars?' his father had shouted. His mother had been out buying him three sets of underclothes, water-purifying tablets and five tubes of anti-dysentery pills.

Four days later he'd been sitting under a palm tree in the oasis surrounding Marrakesh. Twenty yards away a labourer steered a wood-handled plough behind a camel while two more workmen opened the irrigation ditch to allow water to flow out on to the freshly turned earth.

He had overtaken two equally young Americans on the track back to town. They stopped at a café. There, sitting on the terrace with a grapevine sheltering them, glasses of mint tea steaming and a big fat joint passing from hand to hand, his new acquaintances asked his name.

'Pleasure,' he answered.

Neither he nor they had been surprised.

Now, leaning forward, he tested the rice. Lifting the pan off the fire he looked at Patrick.

'We're not so different,' he said.

Patrick smiled. 'How long till you turned dealer?' he asked.

'Four weeks,' Pleasure admitted. He'd strapped a half-pound bag of *kief* between his legs – sold it in Amsterdam.

He shrugged. 'Made my rail fare from Marrakesh.'

Serving half the rice on to a plate for Patrick, he sliced raw onion, leek and chilli into the pot for himself. 'Sorry,' he apologized, as he handed Patrick his dinner. 'Plain rice for two days.'

'Curative or punitive?'

Pleasure laughed. 'Rice binds,' he said.

They ate in silence. Only the splash of the fall broke the stillness of the valley. Already there was frost in the air, cleaning it, magnifying the stars till they seemed to hang just above the mountain peaks.

He passed Patrick the joint, then sat glowering at the fire. Gang! He with his pride that he always worked alone. He bought in kilos, sold in kilos, made his own cases and ran his own risks. Except for once. And then it had been his pride which had messed him up. Ibiza, Spain – September 1971. He'd just talked an American girl out of making a run to Montreal for Danish Pete.

'Man, you really fuck things up,' Pete said.

Pleasure had been lying alone on Salinas beach. That's where the Dane found him.

'So what did I do?' Pleasure asked.

'You know damn well what you did,' Pete said. 'You fucked our trip!'

'Why don't you run your own shit?' Pleasure asked. 'Scared?'

'Fuck, man! You and your crumby little four-kee numbers,' Pete snapped back. 'You don't have the balls for anything big.'

So, two months later, Pleasure found himself driving a car for Pete. From the start the job was a mess. The girl who delivered the car to Málaga turned out to be wanted by the Danish police. That for starters – though they didn't tell Pleasure till just before he left Tangier. Málaga was where he collected the car. They loaded in Morocco.

The loading was no problem except that, when it was finished, the car stank and the linings looked ten years old. The car was new. A Citroen GS.

The plates were Danish commercial and there were no papers in Pleasure's name. Finally Pete got him an International Insurance card and then only because Pleasure insisted. At least *that* had his name on it – or the name on the passport he was using.

Pete swore the stink would go if he drove with the windows

open. Pleasure did. It was winter by then which didn't add much joy to the trip, nor much credibility. By this time Pleasure had been convinced the whole gig was insane. Still, he only had to drive the car as far as Puttgarden in Schleswig-Holstein. Some other idiot would take it across the German-Danish frontier. He hoped a Danish car wouldn't excite much interest till then. He had his hair cut and got ready to go.

He took the North African route. Tangier, Fez, Oran, Algiers, Constantine and Tunis. He caught a boat from Tunis. The boat he'd been told to catch didn't run in winter. He took the ferry to Cagliari in southern Sardinia. The customs there were no problem – the whole lot were outside the gates inspecting a Saturday-night pile up of four small Fiats and a bright red Maserati. The gates were open. Pleasure didn't stop.

He drove north to Olbia through the rest of that night and caught a second ferry over to Civitavecchia which is the port for Rome. By now he was running short of funds which seemed normal for this type of crazy trip. He made Rome to Puttgarden, which is around two thousand kilometres, in twenty-six hours flat. He tried to nap in the car but it was too cold, and he didn't eat more than one sandwich the whole way.

This was money not masochism. Pete had set up an expensive and paranoia-crazed rendezvous which entailed Pleasure having to hire a car in Copenhagen when he arrived. Pete was good at looking after himself. Danish Pete. For all Pleasure knew he might have been a Swede and a Jack or a John or a Niels, but he'd been Danish Pete in Ibiza on and off for five years.

From Puttgarden, there is a car and train ferry over to Rødby in Denmark. The voyage takes an hour. Pleasure left the car in the parking lot. He bought a second-class single to Copenhagen on the train – this included the boat passage – then he boarded. He found a chair in the corner of the lounge, stretched his legs out and fell fast asleep. There weren't many other passengers and there were none when he awoke. He didn't know if he was in Denmark or Germany. Grabbing his bag, he ran out into the lobby. A sailor stood there, scratching his balls through his trouser pockets.

'What's happening?' Pleasure asked.

'Finished,' the sailor told him.

'What's finished? Where are we?' Pleasure wanted to know.

'Train?' a clerk asked, coming out of the closed bank kiosk. Pleasure nodded.

'Down,' the clerk told him.

Pleasure still looked dazed so the sailor led the way. Two minutes later Pleasure found himself being pushed up into the first-class sleeping car of the Scandinavian Express. Pleasure tracked the guard down in his small cubicle at the end of the car. There was an ice box full of beer.

All the American wanted was to know where they were. Was this the Rome-Stockholm train or the Stockholm-Rome? Were they in Rødby or still in Puttgarden? He had no common language with the guard and it was difficult to explain by signs that he didn't know where he was. So they split two beers. By this time the train was off the boat. They were shunted back and forth for five minutes. Then they stopped and Pleasure got off the train. He found a big sign saying Rødby. Relieved, he walked along till he found an empty second-class non-smoker, slung his bag up on the rack, and fell asleep again in the forward-facing corner seat. Somehow he'd evaded both customs and immigration. Two hours later he woke up in Copenhagen.

Pleasure called from the station.

'I'm here,' he said.

That was all. Then he replaced the receiver and walked across the road to the the Hertz office where he hired a VW for one day. This done, he had thirty minutes till the rendezvous. He parked the car at the station. Bought a *Herald Tribune* at the kiosk then walked over to the corner café. He read the funnies over a large cup of black coffee and a schnapps. He badly needed the lift of all three.

He got back to the car with five minutes to spare. Driving slowly, he circled the main square before heading up past the end of the walking street. Pete was standing with Britta on the corner. Britta was one of the Dane's steadies – martyr material as long as the death didn't take too long.

'Welcome,' Pete said, as he pushed Britta in behind the front seat.

The whole pick-up had taken less than thirty seconds.

'Where do we go?' Pleasure asked. Perhaps he should have said thanks, but he wasn't in the mood.

'Keep driving straight,' Pete told him.

They drove out of town along the motorway while Pleasure told the Dane how the trip had gone.

'And where's the car now?' Pete wanted to know.

'Puttgarden,' Pleasure told him, 'like you said.'

'Fine.'

But Pete didn't sound fine.

'We just going to drive all night?' Pleasure asked. 'I haven't eaten for two days and I haven't slept.'

Pete told him to take a right off the motorway. They drove another ten kilometres before stopping at a roadside inn.

'You want to come in too?' Pete asked Britta.

Pleasure turned to look at her as she nodded. He couldn't remember her speaking since she got in the car. He had a strong feeling she hated the whole business . . . on top of which she was obviously scared.

'Who's going to fetch the Citroen?' Pleasure asked.

There was a bad moment's silence then Pete shrugged. 'We'll talk about it,' he said.

'I've done my bit,' Pleasure told him as firmly as he could.

But there was doubt in his voice. He could hear it. He was suddenly sure Pete had Britta set for the job. What a total motherfucker, Pleasure thought. He was out of the VW fast, as if he could escape his suspicions. He couldn't. Something had to explain her fear.

He stood there in the cold with his legs trembling – he was that angry.

'Britta going to drive?' he asked.

Pete shrugged again. 'I told you – we'll talk about it,' he said.

'So what's wrong with now?' Pleasure asked.

'Take it easy, will you?' Pete pleaded. 'Come on, man, let's eat.'

This was Pete's forte – the restaurant scene. An eyebrow raised, the quick snap of his fingers somehow done with charm despite the arrogance, waiters running – the big order from the big man. They had artichokes, followed by steak *au poivre* and then cheese. A dry Chablis with the artichokes, a bottle of Burgundy, then brandy with their coffee, and the bill.

Pleasure didn't see the bill but he knew how much money he had left in his own pockets. Exactly eight Danish kroner, a dollar ten.

'You have my bread?' he asked.

Pete got a pained *let's not talk money in front of the ladies* look on his face. Which were two subjects the Dane was trying to avoid. The picture clicked.

'You're broke,' Pleasure said. 'You're broke and you want me to drive that car, right?'

Pete shrugged. He was very suave. 'I'm never broke,' he said.

'But you don't have my bread.'

'We're pressed,' Pete admitted.

'So I'll wait,' Pleasure told him. 'But there's no way for me to drive that car.' He shook his head slowly and as firmly as he could. 'No way,' he said. 'No way at all. Look.' He passed the Dane his passport. 'No entry stamp.'

'So?'

'Come on,' Pleasure insisted. 'Have some sense of reality, Pete. I go out of here – I get an exit stamp, and then I'm back the same day. There's still no original entry. That's all they need. One suspicion and they'll be on to the car, and the car stinks.'

'We're not discussing the car,' Pete interrupted quickly.

'Why not?' Pleasure demanded.

He was over-aware of Britta sitting there between them. She just kept on watching her plate. That's all she had done ever since they'd been in the restaurant. She had eaten almost nothing and the one glass of wine she'd taken was still half-full.

She looked crumpled, Pleasure thought. Folded in on herself.

'So what's that strange about your brief?' Pleasure heard Pete insist. 'They don't always stamp you for entry.'

'Crap!' Pleasure told him. 'And I've half a dozen North African entries on the same page.' He shrugged suddenly. Looked straight into Pete's eyes. 'She going to drive?' he asked. 'Britta going to drive if I don't?'

'Someone's got to drive.' Pete smiled. 'Of course, if you're nervous . . . ' he said. And they were back on Salinas beach.

Pleasure was getting angry. He felt trapped. 'Come on,' he said, 'let's get the fuck out of here.'

So now they argued in the car. They argued for fifty kilometres. Pete sounded increasingly querulous, Pleasure thought. For himself, he was tired of the whole discussion, tired from the drive, tired. He could feel himself withdrawing behind a barrier of automatic response. One last time he went over the salient points: the unnaturalness of an American driving a Danish car, especially one on commercial plates; the problem of his passport – that lone exit stamp which would draw attention to his North African passage; and lastly that he didn't want to drive the car any further, nor, till he'd arrived, had he ever been asked to.

And Pete's arguments were always the same: they had no money to pay Pleasure till the car was safely through to Stockholm; that Pleasure had got this far, thus proving he was right for the job; that, if he didn't drive, then Britta would; and lastly, but not said, the implication of his refusal coming from cowardice.

Interspersed amongst these arguments came a continual stream of complaints: too much draught from the window, the seats were too hard, there was not enough leg room for a man of Pete's height.

Under pressure the Dane's charm slowly dissolved till Pleasure had the impression he was driving a spoilt child through the night. And in the back sat Britta, always silent.

Pleasure had a growing desire to round on the Dane – cut him with a few home truths. But that would not help. A quarrel now was the last thing they could afford. No, if he was going to chauffeur the shit then what he needed was calm and sleep. But he did not get the sleep, not even after he'd surrendered.

Now Pete fought to draw out of Pleasure a statement of his desire to drive the car – a desire that would absolve Pete from further responsibility. The extent of the Dane's moral cowardice was too total to shock Pleasure. This was Pete's shit. Pete's investment. Pete's car, in whoever's name it might be registered – and, if Pleasure succeeded, it would be Pete's profit. There was no danger for the Dane – only a financial risk which he could soon recoup.

One remark of Pete's that night seemed to sum the whole game up. They'd dropped Britta home, then Pete insisted he and Pleasure go to a club for one last drink. It was already too late for sleep. Pete lolled on a plush red couch with his polished boots stretched way out under the table which, with its load of bottles and glasses, together with the hired car already represented twice the weekly pay packet of a normal working-man (this when Pete was supposedly broke); on either side of him sat a pretty little teenager, each with mouth open and eyes alight, their minds concussed by the blaring sounds and the strobe lights whipping – teenagers waiting to be used.

'I'm a big fish in a small pond,' Pete casually remarked as if the girls were not even there. And you are the small fish, was the implication. Small fish ready for raping. No dope mysticism here: just one more extension of the capitalist world. Dog eat dog, and throw crumbs to the also-rans, if any survive.

All this passed through Pleasure's mind again in the morning as he rode the train back south to Rødby. The continual argument, together with Pleasure's lack of sleep and fatigue from the long drive up from Africa, had forced him back into himself in self-protection. He had no recollection of being so completely introverted since he'd left his parents' house. In his childhood this state had been normal. He'd almost forgotten – leaving home had been the end of the need for self-protection. There had been no slow unfurling – just an instant shattering of the brittle shell, and he'd stepped out free. Now he was back.

The was no joy. He felt as if he'd physically shrunk.

It was five o'clock that afternoon when he picked the car up from the parking lot at Puttgarden ferry terminal. There was no one else in the long glass-sided corridor which led down from the boat to the lobby with its strip-lit bank, ticket office and coffee bar. His boots struck the concrete floor, flinging shards of uncontrollable echo ricocheting on ahead – way on ahead beneath the cold fluorescent lighting to the grey mist outside.

He felt watched and obvious as he walked. His body was heavy, sludgy and springless. His bag dragged his arm. He raised the hood of his duffel-coat as he stepped outside. Rain stung at him. Wind shoved. A police car stood empty by the parking lot.

For a moment he thought the Citroen had gone. There was a brief instant of relief. He could turn. Walk back into the station. Take a train to Hamburg. Telephone Pete from a call-box. Catch the night sleeper south to the sun. But the car was there. With its hydraulics empty, it lay low to the ground in the shadow of a red Bedford panel truck. Muddy and exhausted, it looked, like a scuffed white slug. He hated it – the whole business; the cold wind flecked with rain, the grey miserable dusk, and the car – most of all the car.

He opened the driver's door and flung his bag on to the passenger seat all in one rapid movement. Then he was in, with the key turning the ignition. The engine didn't fire. Paranoia clubbed him. The shit stank. The starter whined and whined like a dentist's drill. He wanted to run. As he pumped the gas pedal, he was certain that he was watched. That the police had found the car. That they'd disconnected the distributor cap.

Calmness, he told himself. Cool down. *Smile!*

The engine caught.

The suspension system filled.

The car rose.

Pleasure switched on the lights. There was so much condensation on the windows, he couldn't see out. Turning on the wipers, he cleaned the inside of the screen with his sleeve.

The result still wasn't good but he wanted to get out of the parking lot and away from under the eyes of the police and the German customs. He wondered if they had dogs. Probably not.

As his foot backed off the clutch, his fear of drawing attention to himself inhibited him from giving the engine enough gas. The motor stalled. Fucking car, he thought, as the starter whined again. This time he was off.

He drove bent forward over the wheel as if being those few inches closer to the screen would help him see. The wipers swished across his view. The wind beat at the car, pushing it sideways. His stomach hurt. For the first time he started to hate them – the organization men – the Petes of the business. Spoilt kids. He hated their flash posturing and their safety. Their ability to make him feel like a male prostitute. That's what they were, *pimps*. Pimps turning women into whores. Pimps living off their women's earnings. Nothing had changed, Pleasure thought, as he drove. Nothing except that, in a world of liberated sex, the pimps had found a new use for women. The rest was the same. The men lolled in the bars and restaurants and night-clubs while the chicks took the risks in the cold outside.

He knew as he drove that the only sensible action would be to park the car. Put the keys in the post. Walk away. But he could not. Inevitability held him to the Citroen. He had no illusions left as he drove. This was no romantic adventure. It was defeat . . . whatever the outcome. He had allowed himself to be used and he had been used not even for profit but simply to feed Pete's vanity. One more power game. Now, like a prostitute, he accepted his role.

It was as simple as that, Pleasure thought, as he drove the Citroen on down the dark grey shiny road with the rain blasting across it and the sure strong stink of hash in his nostrils.

He drove cautiously. An accident would have been the final idiocy. Anyway there was no hurry. Late at night would be safest for the border crossing – late at night and raining. Nothing else to do, he drove south to Oldenberg before turning west. Now the yellow signs pointed his way to Kiel – then Rendsburg, Friedrichstadt, and north to Husum. The streets of the towns were bright with Christmas decorations. Curves of white light-bulbs swooped above him: crowns, pendants, stars; all these and Christmas trees in the village squares, but the streets were deserted.

The fleeting glimpse of a scurrying raincoat was his only contact with humanity; raincoats and the cars which swept past, wrapped in their insulating clouds of spray. It was as if the world had already cut him off and the intended gaiety of the decorations only added to his sense of isolation.

In Husum he ate, then headed north to the border. Fifty kilometres to go. He still drove slowly as if delay could help. He was like a suicide, he thought, a suicide waiting for the tide to come in before throwing himself off the bridge.

Five kilometres short of Süderlügum he drew off the road into the mouth of a farm lane. Here he got out, pissed, changed his trousers for a warmer pair, then tidied the back of the car. He hung the yellow oilskins Pete had bought him that morning over the back of the seat and arranged the half dozen yachting magazines the Dane had given him on the passenger seat. These were meant to be his cover.

'You're up here to buy a boat,' Pete had instructed him.

'In mid-winter?'

'Sure, they're cheaper,' the Dane told him.

'And what was I doing in Africa?' Pleasure had asked. 'Also boats?'

But this was history, he thought, as he arranged his bag and the golf clubs he'd brought with him and the chess board and the two tartan blankets. He was kneeling there in the back of the Citroen when a German police car circled from the other side of the road to halt across his escape from the lane. In a moment the police were out. Their flash-lights blinded him.

What was he doing?

Where was he going?

Where did he come from?

Pleasure explained that he'd stopped to urinate and to

change into warmer clothes.

The police laughed, checked the inside of the car quickly with their lamps, then with a wish of 'good trip', they were off back the way they had come.

An omen, Pleasure wondered as he settled back into the driving seat. And if so, for good or for bad?

Twice on the way to Flensburg he lost the road. Each time he found himself on a route south to Hamburg and safety. He was stupid to turn back and knew he was stupid. And then leaving Flensburg with only eight kilometres left to the border, he was wrong again but this time on the autobahn.

He drove south at a steady ninety kilometres an hour. He passed two turn-offs. The big blue signs beckoned him to safety. Hamburg ... Hamburg. But in the end he had not the courage to be a coward. He turned north to the border. The Germans waved him straight through. Then Denmark.

As Pleasure handed up his passport through the car window to the controller, all his arguments with Pete resurfaced.

An American driving a Danish car?

An American with a Danish exit stamp of that day but with no previous entry stamp?

Then they would look closer. There on the same page were all those North African entries – Morocco – Algeria – Tunisia.

Pleasure knew he was down. He didn't have to watch the second passport officer join the first in the brightly lit kiosk. Nor did he have to wonder what would happen at the customs barrier. He knew, and it happened exactly as he'd always known it would from the moment Pete had begun to pressure him.

There was no hesitation on the part of the customs. They waved him straight through to the garage and the heavy search routine. They were polite. Their questions were polite and they were the questions he'd known they would ask. He was no longer nervous – certainly not afraid. It was too late for fear. Now there could be no emotion except acceptance. He obediently followed the senior customs officer who led him through into an office to wait.

Muffled in his duffel-coat, he sat there with Pete's yachting magazines on his knees. They had been bought as his disguise. Now they contained only dreams. Idly he sketched a small fishing boat on a pad of buff forms lying on the desk. First the hull with its sweeping sheer. Then the mast, the gaff-hung mainsail, the staysail, and the jib. He looked at the drawing for a while before adding the comfort of a small wheelhouse.

The customs officer watched. 'All?' he asked.

Pleasure nodded.

The officer turned the drawing and took the pen from Pleasure's hand. He studied the little boat for a while then shrugged and drew in, behind the wheelhouse, a low mizen with a marconi sail. Both men smiled. Pleasure was tired but curiously content. They would find the hashish, he had no doubt of that. But in a strange way he recognized that he had arrived where he wanted to be. For the first time since he'd been involved with Pete he felt fully human. He was free. Prison was a minor obstacle.

The customs officer was talking to him, searching clumsily for the English words. It was as if this ageing official had sensed Pleasure's thoughts.

'My teacher,' he told the American. 'My schoolteacher, he teached us a man's dream must be a small fish boat, a house, a small land.' The Dane's hands gestured the size. 'One field; a cow, pigs, a few chickens.'

Pleasure nodded. The door opened. The overalled searcher stuck his head into the office. He had a screwdriver in one hand. He spoke briefly to his chief and was gone.

'So,' the customs officer told Pleasure. 'They find it.'

He did not sound pleased . . . more tired than anything. He picked up the drawing they'd made, looked at it once more, then dropped it into the bin under his desk. Glancing up at Pleasure, he shrugged. There was nothing more to say.

'Except that I served nineteen months,' Pleasure told Patrick. He threw half a dozen sticks on to the fire before looking at the Irishman. Patrick had not moved while Pleasure told his story.

94

'How was it?' he asked now.

'Jail? Not bad,' Pleasure said. 'The food was edible, the heating worked and the warders weren't pigs or anything. For the rest, I don't know what jails are for.'

Perhaps no one did, he thought. Revenge? Punishment? Cure? The jail he'd been in had not been vengeful and the only vicious punishment was for those outside: prisoners' wives suffered and their kids ended up with minds choked by fear and hate, so creating a new generation of criminals.

'The whole system's self-defeating,' he told Patrick. 'Most crime is fantasizing yourself out of a situation you can't deal with – right? If your crime comes off you've got the bread. If you fail, you're protected. They put you in a cell where no one can get at you: no rent collector, no boss screaming at you, no more job you're scared you can't hold down. You're safe and there's no one to destroy your dreams.' He shrugged. Lit a cigarette.

'That's what a cell is,' he said. 'A fantasy box.'

'Like hard drugs,' Patrick murmured. 'But without the risk of death.'

Pleasure looked up, surprised. 'Huh?'

For a moment Patrick looked embarrassed. He smiled. 'So I'm a narco – that mean I'm not allowed to think?' he asked. 'Crime wave, drug wave, alcoholics, pill heads, TV addicts – we're all trying to clamber into dream worlds.' He shrugged. 'All that's crazy is we try to cure each other instead of trying to cure the world that's driving us all nuts.' His smile broadened. 'Talking of dreams, you want to roll us another joint?'

Pleasure laughed. 'That's the next charge I'll have against me – corrupting a narco.'

'Mostly I'm a lush,' Patrick said as he watched Pleasure crumble hash into a palm of tobacco.

'Bad?' Pleasure asked.

'Getting that way,' Patrick admitted. 'You ever try junk?'

'Snorted it a couple of times,' Pleasure answered. 'Fixed once. It's not my trip. What for?' he asked. 'I dig life so why die?'

He lit the joint. Blew out a stream of smoke. Grinned at Patrick over the glowing tip. 'Even with you following me,' he said and passed the joint.

Patrick inhaled. 'Nor ever run it?' he asked.

'Shit, no! Would you push junk?'

'There's cops who have.' Patrick took another drag. Then sat watching the flames for a while. Finally he looked up.

'I guess it's the bread,' he said. 'In the end it gets to some of us. Twenty thousand dollars for a kilo of smack. Year after year you're writing reports on that sort of bread. Can you imagine?' he asked.

Pleasure grinned. 'Cops and Mafia. You're the pros.'

Patrick passed him the joint. 'A few of each,' he said.

'While amateurs deal dope.'

'Or moralists,' Patrick murmured into the fire. 'Ever think of yourself like that?' he asked. 'Think of the work. A kilo of smack's worth more profit than twenty kees of hash – no smell, fully soluble. Why else do you do it? Or are you just plain crazy?'

'Morals is why you don't push junk,' Pleasure admitted. He took another drag at the cigarette. The dope was beginning to float his head. Suddenly he chuckled. 'Know where it's really at?' he asked. 'Running dope? It's a gas. That's where it's at. The bread doesn't matter. It's the adrenalin kick while you make the run. Then turning the heads on to the best hash in town.' He held up the smouldering butt.

'Look at it,' he said. 'No evil, just a gas.'

Patrick grinned. 'That's what I like,' he told Pleasure. 'Product loyalty . . . and I'm for the trees.'

Watching him go, Pleasure got up and spread their bags. He piled the fire up high. Scratched the back of his head. Made another joint.

'Time for a pill,' he reminded Patrick, as the Irishman came back to the fire. 'Then bed.'

'And tomorrow?' Patrick asked.

Pleasure shrugged. Sitting on his bag, he pulled off his boots and socks, shed his pants and clambered in. There ought to be problems, he thought.

There were none . . . or none he could see.

'You don't like it here,' he said.

'Too right I don't,' Patrick assured him.

'And I'm broke.' It was too beautiful, Pleasure thought. Too perfect. Smoke trickled up from the joint towards the stars. To their east, the moon sat smiling on the mountain ridge. The moon was always good, he mused. He'd always made his runs at full moon . . . except that one for Danish Pete. Full moon shining in through the aeroplane window – that was another part of the kick.

Rolling over on his side to face the Irishman, he held out the joint. 'You want to move?' he murmured. 'Then you'll have to pay the cheque.' He grinned. 'What have you got to lose?' he asked. 'You follow me because you're with me or you follow me because you're following me. Either way you follow me and my way you won't get lost.'

Patrick accepted the joint. He took a deep drag. Held the smoke down for as long as he could. Then whistled it out.

'You motherfucker,' he said. He flicked the butt into the flames. 'Total goddam motherfucker – right?'

'Right,' Pleasure happily agreed. Lying there looking up at the Irishman, he tried to contain his mirth.

And Patrick attempted to keep his own face straight. No chance. The hash seemed to melt his muscles. Grinning like an idiot, he slowly shook his head.

'Motherfucker!' he swore again . . . and began to laugh. He had to sit down. Then lie down. His legs waved weakly at the moon. The moon laughed back. There were extra joints all through his limbs. Rubber body. He tried to look at his companion. Tried to see through his tears. Gave up. Lay flat on his back.

'God!' he gasped. 'Where am I . . . and where in hell will we go?'

'It's not dealer's choice,' Pleasure reminded him. 'We go, it's on your bread.'

BOOK TWO

'Havens are high priced. The price exacted of the haven-dweller is that he contrive to delude himself into believing that he has found a haven.'

James Baldwin

CHAPTER ONE

Layer upon layer of stone gods and gopies danced, clambered and fornicated their way to the summit of the temple gopura. The wedge-shaped tower was newly painted, the garish colours powdery – like make-up, Patrick thought. Make-up plastered over raddled skin.

This close to noon there was no shade. He was hot and tired. Guide-book to India in hand, he tried to ignore both flies and the small boy who dragged at his sleeve.

'Please, Sahib,' the child begged. 'This way, Sahib.'

Sweat stinging his eyes, Patrick shook his head.

'Please, Sahib . . . '

'Go away,' Patrick pleaded.

The child sensed weakness. 'Krishna fucking,' he tempted the American. 'I show.'

Patrick headed for the gate. A scab-plastered beggar thrust his bowl out. Patrick stepped back. His right foot struck flesh. He glanced down. A limbless man lay in the dust. The hollow of his crushed rib-cage cupped five small coins. Flies crawled over his mouth and across the white-scaled pupils of his eyes. Patrick fled.

Slamming open the door to their room in the government rest-house, he leant panting against the wall. Pleasure rested propped up on his bed with a notebook open on his knees. Six piles of bills lay on the table beside him together with a jug of iced lime. A trace of cannabis scented the air. He looked cool and contented.

'How was the temple' he asked.

'Like a wedge of maggoty cheese.' Patrick flung the guide-book on to his own bed. 'I've had enough,' he said.

'Relax,' Pleasure told him. They'd been together four weeks: one week in Kabul while Patrick recovered from dysentery, a week in Pakistan, and now two weeks sightseeing in India.

'You've seen more temples in a fortnight than I've seen in nine years,' Pleasure added.

Patrick shrugged. 'What in hell else is there to do?'

'Relax,' Pleasure repeated. 'You're going at things too fast.'

Patrick collected the jug of lime then crossed to the dresser on which stood a rum bottle beside three glasses on a brass tray. His back to Pleasure, he poured himself a stiff drink. He held his glass cupped in both hands as he walked through to the bathroom.

Pleasure lay listening to the shower run. Then he glanced at the dresser. Two days unsealed, the rum bottle was nearly empty.

'Want a joint?' he asked as Patrick came back in.

Shaking his head, the Irishman returned to the dresser. Glass replenished, he lay down.

'What about food?' Pleasure suggested.

'You're getting to sound like a male nurse,' Patrick complained. 'And what in hell are you doing with those bills?'

Pleasure grinned. 'Your expense account,' he said. 'Here.' He threw Patrick the notebook.

Patrick glanced at it. 'Scared I'll lose my job?' he snapped.

He reached out for the pack of Marlboro Pleasure had left on the table between their beds. 'Nine years,' he said. 'How can you keep on coming back?'

'You have to take India easy,' Pleasure explained. 'Dip into it for what you want to see then break for cover.'

'So where's the cover?'

'Nepal, Kashmir . . . '

'In mid-winter!'

Pleasure shrugged.

'And Goa,' Patrick prompted. 'I thought that was where you all went for Christmas?'

'That's the trip,' Pleasure agreed.

'So?'

Pleasure shrugged again. 'No temples,' he said.

'And that's meant to put me off?'

Pleasure smiled. 'I guess not,' he admitted. Getting up, he walked through to the bathroom. Urinated. Came back.

'Because I'm a narco,' Patrick greeted him. 'Right?'

Glancing down at the watch on Patrick's wrist, 'You want to eat?' Pleasure asked.

'Screw eating!'

'So what do you want me to say?'

Patrick stubbed out his cigarette. Reached for his glass. Drained it. 'It's not saying anything,' he said. 'It's trusting. And I don't mean me. You have to trust yourself. You're scared,' he accused. 'Scared of seeing the way you live through the way you think I'll see you.' Hand on the bottle. 'Or do you just think I'm a rat?' he asked.

'Friendship or duty,' Pleasure told him.

'A rat either way?'

Pleasure walked over to his bed. There were two ready-rolled joints tucked under his pillow. He lit one before lying down. The electric fan turned slowly above his head. And then the cream-painted ceiling, fly-specked and stained with damp. 'That's about the size of it,' he said. He heard the clink of glass on glass as his companion poured himself the last of the rum.

'You ever own a dog?' the Irishman asked.

Pleasure shook his head.

'I had one in Vietnam,' Patrick told him. 'Any time he had a problem he'd get his head down and lick his joint.' He ducked. The pillow Pleasure shied at him hit the wall. Patrick grinned. 'He wasn't much of a dog,' he said, 'but he was fun to have around.'

'I'm to put that against the years you've been a narco?' Pleasure asked. 'See what I mean?' Taking a deep drag on his cigarette, he held the smoke down in his lungs while he thought. 'If it was me,' he said and the smoke steamed up at the ceiling to be torn to shreds by the fan. 'If it was me, I wouldn't care. It's my family. They'll be in Goa.' He rolled over on to his side to look at Patrick.

The Irishman raised his glass in a silent toast. 'So?'

'So I'm not the only one of us who deals dope,' Pleasure pointed out. 'Some of us run ten. Some of us run fifty. Now and again there's a group enterprise and a hundred-kee number gets put together.'

'Never junk?'

'You're kidding!' Pleasure exploded. 'I never even met a pusher till I got stuck in jail.' He pulled fresh smoke down into his lungs. 'Look,' he suggested, 'we'll make a deal. We go to Kashmir and I'll score some hash.' He nodded at the accounts he'd been preparing. 'We've the bread for five. Then it's your choice. You get me busted when I've scored if that's where your head's at . . . or we go to Goa and you lay off my friends. Right?' he asked and studied Patrick through a curtain of exhaled cannabis.

'Right,' Patrick agreed. 'If you trust me that far?'

'I've been trusting people all my life,' Pleasure told him. 'No other way in my business unless you're into carrying a gun.' Feeling suddenly loose with the dope, 'Trusting – that's fifty per cent of the kick,' he said, and smiled.

CHAPTER TWO

November in Kashmir. Pleasure sat waiting on the small verandah of the houseboat they'd rented for a week. Around him spread the reeds and the lake. Ice by the shore, farther out the water lay totally still – a slate plane, metallically smooth, which slid into the surrounding mist like the blade of a scythe. The mountains were guessed at – barely perceptible thickenings of the mist; a blue hint in the soft grey.

Now, at noon, the sun appeared as a pale-yellow disk into which he could stare without blinking. The windows and glass-paned sliding doors to the verandah reflected what little heat survived the filter of cold humidity.

From within came the tin clatter of Ghulam, the houseboat owner, stoking the stoves. Patrick slept on. At least he was now silently asleep. His rum-heavy snores had continued well into the morning. Alcohol was a drag, Pleasure thought, as he watched a skiff slip out from behind the rushes to his left. A small boy knelt upright in the bows. His paddling was automatic; his breath rhythmic pants which left puffs of drifting condensation . . . a steam-driven toy, Pleasure mused . . . . Heads stayed silent when stoned out, dope leaving them content to drift from dream to dream; drunks got cantankerous, boring or tragic – on top of which, apart from being easier to buy, this had to be the one area of the world where hash came cheaper than booze.

Patrick refused to accept their problem – that there were two of them. Despite the adage, two could not live as cheaply as one. Pleasure knew. He had spent two more hours that morning working the receipts for their combined lives into a passable expense account for the Irishman to forward to his office. He hadn't finished. His bed lay strewn with indecipherable scraps of paper – confetti for the wedding which had made him the man of the house. Despite his anxiety, Pleasure smiled. But left to Patrick, he knew the accounts would never get done – or not so long as the rum held out.

They should have gone to a dry state . . . though Goa would be all right with palm toddy at a few cents the bottle. If they got to Goa. But that was Patrick's problem; or decision. His own was either to help the Irishman pull himself together or to end up writing reports on dope just to keep Patrick his job. And the Irishman needed his job. Without it, he had nothing to occupy his mind – or nothing good. He'd lost all enthusiasm. Down on the plains he'd visited the temples and museums. Here he did nothing . . . except drink, Pleasure thought, and, feeling uncomfortably responsible, looked down at the shikari boat which waited at the foot of the verandah steps to take him buying.

The pleated curtains surrounding the passenger seat hung limp with cold. Patterned with entwined red roses, these cotton frills seemed to Pleasure as scandalously inappropriate to this winter noon as the boatman's bare feet which poked out from beneath the hem of the Kashmiri's tweed *jellum*. Their eyes met. Numb-faced, the boatman nodded at the approaching skiff.

The skiff turned in towards the houseboat. The boy swayed from side to side as he forced the flat bows up over the ice. He also was barefoot, Pleasure saw. The rocking thrust ripples under the ice, cracking it and widening the passage. Ghulam came out on to the verandah. He carried a rug over his arm and a wicker-bound clay firepot in each hand.

Seeing the houseboat owner, the boy shouted what sounded to Pleasure like an explanation.

Satisfied, 'You may go now,' Ghulam told the American. 'All is prepared.'

Shedding his shoes, Pleasure stepped down into the shikari

boat. Ghulam passed him the firepots. With these between his legs and the rug draped over his shoulders, the American settled himself like a pasha amongst the cushions beneath the flowered canopy.

Out in the lake they turned right towards the canals which threaded the miles of market garden surrounding the Kashmiri capital of Srinagar. To their left lay a small island from which punts supporting rush-mat tents fanned out like the brass leaves of a Moroccan choker. Smoke seeped through the matting while, bulky with layered skirts, women squatted cooking in the open bows, an eye to their children – these children playing bare-legged under the trees from which hung cobwebs of fishing net sprinkled with ice ... villagers driven from their up-country farms by that summer's drought.

The boatman took the right-hand canal leading north from the capital. They passed a baker paddling lakewards. Two deep baskets of fresh bread perched on a platform behind him. Covered with check cloths to retain their warmth, the piled loaves left a scented trail down which Pleasure's boatman steered. A bean salesman and a butcher glided by – these with their punts mounted with brass scales hung from hooks on wooden gallows.

There were birds everywhere: flocks of duck herded by children in half-sized canoes; grey-headed crows, fisher hawks, magpies, sparrows, kingfishers large and small. A woman in rubber boots and apron stood calf-deep beating laundry against a wooden pile. A small girl wearing a red headscarf paddled her bearded grandfather who squatted dead centre in their boat with a water pipe held steady between his feet.

The land was cut by side streams into narrow strips which sprouted regiments of winter leeks and onions. The houses were three and four storeys high, their roofs steep pitched, their walls timber-latticed brick. Windows were boarded or glazed with plastic sheeting. Glass panes were a rarity seen only in the tourist shops attached to workrooms: *Kashmiri Handicrafts Emporium, Oriental Apiary, Ali's Shawls and Sari Museum, Chaku's Woodwork Palace.*

The earth banks of the canal were bound by roots of willow trees whose branches arched the water so that they glided down a woven tunnel. A fat-tailed ram stood tethered at the head of a flight of stone steps leading to an abandoned Hindu temple. Supported by stilts, an open-fronted stall stuck out from the bank. Within sat the owner, cross-legged and smoking, surrounded by open sacks of beans, lentils and rice. This was a Moslem world, alive with vivacious children. There were no soft apathetic Hindu eyes to watch their passing – no beaten, half-starved millions. However harsh the life, it was met without surrender.

The canal widened to their left. Huge tree-trunks floated chained together in the water. A half-built houseboat sat on a covered slipway beside which were logs set ready for sawing on high trestles. No machines, the planks were sawn by hand. Men worked in pairs. One stood on a log, another underneath. They worked in baggy cotton pants and armless undershirts. Still they sweated. The long wood-handled saws ripped through the wood to fill the air with the resin scent of pine and sweeter cedar. The houseboat rang with the tattoo of mallet striking chisel.

Here Pleasure's boatman swung the bow of the shikari boat down a side canal. A signboard jutted from the doorway of a house: *Muhamed's Leatherwork Industry*. A young boy sat watching for them. Pleasure slipped his shoes on. Brief-case hidden under the rug, he leapt ashore and ran up the steps into the shelter of the doorway. Glancing back, he was satisfied to see the boatman paddling impassively on down the canal. Winter was a dangerous time to score. There were too few tourists for anonymity and a shikari boat was easily traced. A bad tourist season and failed harvest could lead to denunciation however little the reward.

The door gave directly on to a small workroom, warm and heavily perfumed with leather. A middle-aged Kashmiri greeted Pleasure. This was Muhamed, whom Ghulam had brought to the houseboat the previous morning. His father squatted in a U-shaped work space watched by an elderly farmer who rose now to meet the foreigner. They exchanged salaams while Muhamed called the boy to fetch tea from the women's quarters.

Crouching beside the father, Pleasure admired his work. The workbench was only a foot higher than the dung floor. On one side a slot held upright a row of hand-made chisels, knives and scrapers. Within the U of this workbench the old man rested on a nest of discarded leather scraps ... a grey owl, Pleasure thought, as he watched the craftsman's fingers pry thread through a lady's purse. The stitch was neat, the work clean and careful. He'd do, Pleasure saw at once. Now all depended on the farmer's goods. These would be proffered in due course. First the ritual tea must be drunk.

Glasses were brought on a cedar-wood tray. Then came the samovar. The boy served his elders before retiring to a corner to prepare their pipe. He took charcoal from beneath the samovar and green tobacco from the old man's pouch. Twice the pipe circled the room. The glasses were refilled. Now it was time.

From beneath his robe the farmer drew a polythene bag which he passed to Pleasure. The contents were like salted rope ends, grey and rock hard. This was Kashmiri twist, the cannabis flowers wrapped in damp cloth wrung tight and left to dry in the sun. However good, it was too difficult to pack, so seldom seen outside the valley. Pleasure sniffed it politely, then scraped a grain free to lay on his tongue.

'You like it?' Muhamed asked.

Pleasure nodded. Twist was these men's daily smoke. Too quick a refusal would offend. 'Excellent,' he approved. 'A fine quality. We never see this in the West.'

As Muhamed translated, the farmer smiled with pleasure.

'Will it do?' Muhamed asked.

'There is a problem,' Pleasure explained. 'Look.' He opened his brief-case to display the lining. 'We must pack this,' he told them. 'Whatever I buy must press thin and flat.'

Nodding his comprehension, the farmer produced a second bag. This time it was black Kashmiri, ebony balls which, heated, could be moulded. Again Pleasure smelt and tasted. The quality was good and he said so.

'Let us smoke,' Muhamed suggested.

While the boy prepared the hashish, Muhamed added water to the samovar. They smoked gently. Sipped tea. This was not the Afghani way. There was no challenge. The atmosphere was ruminative. Conversation grew slowly out of isolated remarks. First the failure of the harvest. Then the Indo-Pakistan war and its disastrous effect on the tourist industry of this Indian border state.

'Even if they are not frightened of a new war,' the father asked, 'what foreigner wishes to visit an army camp?'

The pipe circled as Muhamed translated. Now they talked of the political situation. When would Mrs Ghandi allow freedom for the Kashmiri leaders?

'Twenty years we wait for the promised plebiscite,' the farmer complained. 'The Hindus invaded Bangladesh to free it from Pakistan yet here they allow us no say in our own government.'

'Hindu pigs!' Muhamed spat. 'Their own rajahs the Indians have dispossessed yet claim us as Indian because our rajah was Hindu.' Hands raised to the ceiling, 'How can we fight them?' he pleaded indignantly of a deaf God. 'We who are without friends. Pakistan is defeated and here even to talk of freedom is to be imprisoned.'

'Hypocrisy and corruption,' Pleasure murmured; these the two indispensible words in any discussion of Indian politics. Head drifting with the drug, he lowed softly, his hands sketching the outline of a gross udder. 'Mrs Ghandi,' he explained. He looked first to the two older men, then back to Muhamed. 'The Holy Cow with milk for sale – Brahmins only. Bitch!' he added and sank back against the whitewashed wall as if washed there by the rolling waves of Muhamed's laughter.

'Eee!' the Kashmiri cried and coughed with the tears glistening in his eyes. 'Good! Good!' And now the old men laughed too as Muhamed translated.

The boy crumbled fresh hashish into the bowl of the pipe,

bringing it first to the American.

'Freedom,' Pleasure toasted as he accepted the mouthpiece. 'Freedom for a united Kashmir.' He drew leisurely, the water bubbling gently as the cooled fumes flooded his lungs. A softer smoke than Afghani, he mused ... but good. 'Very good,' he said out loud and looked up to see the farmer produce from the hot shelter of his armpit a large golden ball.

'Pahelgham,' Muhamed whispered in awe. Pahelgham, the rocky hillside famous throughout the Kush and Himalayan foothills for this rare and honey-coloured pollen. Warm with body heat, the ball of hashish was as soft and malleable as Plasticine, its perfume thick with dreams.

'A gift,' Muhamed translated as the farmer handed the ball to Pleasure. 'A gift to friendship and in memory of Kashmir.'

The farmer had intended presenting this pure pollen to the mullah of his family mosque. Now it was Pleasure's. The American knew of Pahelgham as a small-town wine merchant has heard of Imperial Tokay. But to hold it in his hand! 'I can't just take it,' he protested.

'You must,' Muhamed insisted.

'Then may I give something in return?'

To this Muhamed acquiesced. 'But not money,' he warned the American. 'Tomorrow we will decide. I will come to the houseboat. Now the shoes.'

He returned to the workroom carrying a well polished pair of heavy brown brogues. Pleasure kicked off his own shoes. The brogues slipped on easily. A size too large, he thought, as he stood up. The height of the soles built up inside the uppers reminded him of Ibiza – of wearing high-heeled Spanish boots. Exaggerated by his smoking, the sadness of exile dropped as a dark cloak over his previous delight at the farmer's gift – a sadness which showed in his eyes, to be misconstrued by Muhamed.

'They don't fit?' the Kashmiri asked anxiously.

With a quick shake of his head as if to free it, 'They fit,' Pleasure answered. 'They fit well.' Sitting down, he handed the brogues to the father and watched the old man pry delicately with a curved knife at the base of the welt. The lower sole and heel came loose. The old man passed the shoes back to the American.

Pleasure ran a finger round the inside of the exposed cavity.

'Half a kilo,' Muhamed guaranteed.

Plus two in the brief-case – two thousand dollars profit, Pleasure calculated. Or three months' jail. Patrick's decision. 'I'm sorry,' he said. He shook his head again and reached for the pipe. The depression lifted.

There was no romance to Patrick's awakening. Ghulam's eldest son edged open the sliding door. He tiptoed on bare feet to the stove. Lifted the lid without sound. Eased three fresh logs on to the embers. Replaced the lid. Satisfied, he turned to check that Patrick slept. At this moment the Irishman rolled on to his back. Then he snored – only once, but this was enough. The young Kashmiri leapt back. His foot caught the wood pile. Logs cascaded down against the tin side of the stove. The boy fled.

Bolt upright, his heart screaming, Patrick sat staring wildly about the cabin. He had no immediate recollection of where he was. When he did remember, the knowledge in no way alleviated the migraine which threatened to tear his head apart. He wanted to scream – would have, but for his fear that the pain inflicted by fresh sound would surpass the relief of yelling. The time was 3 p.m.

He was half standing when Ghulam peered tentatively round the partly open door. 'Breakfast, Sahib? Coffee?'

Patrick nodded without enthusiasm. 'Where's Pleasure?' he asked.

'Pleasure *Sahib* out, Sahib.'

How many reproofs were there in that short statement, Patrick wondered, as he stumbled to the bathroom. Alone with another day to kill, he thought, slamming the door. Then he cursed at the noise he'd made. Another day without future . . . that was the trouble, he mused, as he lowered himself into the tub; once the future was gone there was little point to the present. Nothing to plan for, nothing to learn for, you were left

112

with yourself and an empty here and now; the here and now worshipped by the heads . . . *Dig it, man! Now's where it's at.*

Which was cool just so long as you kept sufficiently stoned not to notice yourself squatting ugly as a bullfrog in the middle of the mystic Now. Stoned or drunk. Anything to sustain the dream of something outside yourself. Anaesthetize the ego.

In the end there was little difference between booze and hash except that alcohol left you with guilt, a hangover and a fucked-up liver.

Guilt was the drag. More so than the pointlessness. Lying there in the bath he felt suddenly angry. Irrationally bitter. Jealous. *Where in hell was Pleasure? He always had something to do.* Only the dealers had purpose. Was that why they dealt, Patrick wondered. The idea of asking Pleasure made him feel slightly less disconsolate.

He did not shave. He looked at himself in the mirror. Then at his hands. That was enough. He needed coffee. Out in the saloon he sat alone and bored. The toast was too thick, too damp; wedges of cotton wool which threatened to choke him till he finally left the table to spit the unswallowable mess into the lake.

He had nothing of his own to read. The saloon bookshelves offered little: three volumes of historic photographs; historic of the tourist industry. Ghulam as a small boy holding up for admiration a string of eight trout beside an English Colonel Sahib who stood sternly glowering at the lens with his two-piece split-cane fly rod held like an assagai. Ghulam at heel to the Colonel's Mem – here he held a picnic basket. Ghulam steadying the heads of two fat ponies on which the Colonel Sahib's two children sat terrified at the ages of three and five, saddles splaying their legs out like the ball-jointed limbs of plastic dolls. Ghulam again in attendance to the children though this time the children stood beside a mountain stream in outsize sun-helmets; khaki-topped toadstools – poor kids, Patrick thought, as he turned to pages of an older Ghulam guiding two elasticated Mems with starched hair who had to have come from some Christian Mission on the plains. Page after page after page – so few smiles for the camera in these fading memories of the British Raj – so few smiles and so many clothes.

Even the glimpse of a naked wrist dared the emergence of immoral thoughts. Not sexual immorality, for of that there'd been plenty. Female sallies down from the wicked cool of the hill stations to the plains cantonments for sweaty nights of desperate seduction in which the Mems forced copulation out of malaria-sick husbands for proof of parentage. No, not sexual immorality but a more dangerous evil: the idea that these pictured rulers and their families might actually be human, and so, destructible.

Skin emerged during the Second World War, for by then the Japanese had conquered Burma, Malaya and Singapore – dead was the illusion of European immortality. Now there were pages of red knees and rolled-up shirt sleeves, bulging muscles begging for acceptance as proof of masculine authority.

The first Indian Colonel Sahib appeared – a retrogressive step. Tweed hacking jacket, jodhpurs and trout-fly infested cap again banished skin, though now it was the sun these new rulers feared, the further darkening of a faintly brown skin which would threaten the Eastern conception of caste and beauty. 'Wheaten complexion essential,' announced the marriage advertisements in the *Hindu Times*. No joy in these pages, Patrick thought, as he replaced the photographic chronicles.

Fauna and Flora of the Himalayas, Jock of the Bushveldt, Black Beauty, Memoirs of a Foxhunting Man, a volume of Kipling's verse. He opened the Kipling:

> Now is the utmost ebb of night
> When mind and body sink,
> And loneliness and gathering fright
> O'erwhelm us if we think . . . *

Managing a tired smile, Patrick left the book open on the table and turned to look at the clock ticking quietly as a time-bomb

* From 'With Drake in the Tropics'

114

above the dresser — four o'clock in the afternoon. Lone survivor, a two-thirds empty bottle of rum waited below the clock. Pouring himself the first drink of the day, he crossed to the armchair furthest from the table where the book of poetry lay. No sound came from the lake nor from the houseboat . . . or none but the clock's slow tick and the uneven beat of his own heart. A prison, he thought, as he stared morosely out at the still, grey water and the mist. And his office in Frankfurt another prison. A life of prisons in which he worked to imprison others — caterers to cripples, he decided as he returned to the sideboard for the bottle, no water, no ice.

Half an hour later the bottle was empty. He walked through to the bathroom to pee while wondering whether to shave. The ballcock jammed. Something to do, he mocked himself; he placed the cistern lid on the floor. The wire connecting the valve had rusted through. He bent the remainder into place before returning to his bedroom for an overcoat. Looking back into the bathroom he saw himself in the mirror, an unshaved tramp in stolen clothes . . . and a stolen office, he thought. He called to Ghulam for the shikari boat to take him to town in search of company.

Pleasure sat cross-legged and muffled in the shikari boat. With night the mist had cleared. Full moon, the cold had created a clarity which magnified every detail of the canal. A skin of ice lay gleaming on the water so that they glided down a willow wand tunnel to the tinkling of fairy bells. Magic beauty, Pleasure thought. He had no idea whether to sing or cry. The emotion of the farmer's gift had returned to hold him enthralled. To be chased for this, he mused, as they slid out into the lake.

Here there was no ice. To the south-east the moon hung above the mountain wall drawing a golden avenue across the open water. The wooden paddle knocked gently against the side of the skiff; dipped, rose; spattered streamers of moon reflected jewels back into the lake.

They rounded the fishing islet. Lanterns glowed softly from

behind the matting curtains. Smoke scented the air; trickled in lingering grey tendrils across the lattice-screen of trees. Murmur of hushed voices. Outline of a man squatting alone in the bows of his boat, his hawk face held open to the moonlight. Poverty banished by beauty . . . evil, Pleasure wondered? Evil to draw such joy out of the harshness of these people's lives?

As if in answer to his questioning, the silence was suddenly shredded. Guitars cracked electric chords into jagged shards. A tenor sax lost control, its pig squeal tearing at the peace of the night. A youth screamed into a microphone . . . all this from the direction of their houseboat.

'Quick!' Pleasure urged the boatman and turned to watch the Kashmiri bend his head into the fury of sound.

The lake awake, Pleasure fought to control his anger. The lunacy of Patrick! How goddam uncool could you get!

As the skiff touched the houseboat, Pleasure was out and up the steps to the verandah. He carried both pairs of shoes in one hand and his brief-case in the other. The brief-case and brogues he hid in the right-side bench locker at the top of the steps. Still carrying his own shoes, he crossed to the door. No one had heard him. The music was so loud he couldn't hear himself. Furious, he stood looking at the scene.

His back to the door and a half-empty bottle of Indian rum at his elbow, Patrick was playing cards with two freaks. The scent of warm molasses mixed with smoke welcomed Pleasure as he slid the door open. The music came from a portable Sony cassette recorder. Wrapped in a thick rug, a third freak lay shivering on the sofa. He was in his early twenties, thin and pale. Dirt and sweat oozed along the folds of his neck like chocolate sandwich filling. There were pools of sweat collected in his cheekbowls. A pale green junkie skull with the shakes.

'You goddam maniac!' Pleasure shouted.

Two steps got him to the table. He grabbed for the bottle. Sent it curving out through the open door.

'You crazy?' he demanded. 'I can hear that thing halfway down the fucking lake.'

He reached for the Sony. Shut it off. Then looked back at

Patrick who sat sodden and sulky, silent at the table.

'Well?' Pleasure demanded.

No one answered. An oval burn marked the varnished table top – a burn that had to have come from a heated spoon. This was the final straw.

'You,' snapped Pleasure at the two freaks, 'out! And take that thing with you.' He jabbed a thumb at the sofa. 'There's a boat outside. Use it.'

'Now wait a minute . . . ' This from Patrick, who had finally found energy enough to protest – but not to get up. Ignored, his voice drifted off into mumbled complaints; scraps of disconnected monologue just heard through the clumsy efforts of the three junkies to collect their possessions and leave.

They gave no argument. They'd been dispossessed too often. Now they moved where they were pushed with no energy for anything other than the daily ritual of pharmacy, spoon, tie and needle. They had no need to protest. No need to do anything but give Pleasure that quiet, saintly, superior, impenetrable junkie smile which made him hate them all the more; the smile which set them up as the chosen few with everyone else scared of dying, scared of death.

Junkies lived with death. They were only scared of living, Pleasure thought. They moved so slowly that even their actions seemed renunciations of life. Stick-thin arms sketched skeletal shadows across the cedar panelling of the saloon – giant-sized praying manti drawing patterns of an inch-slow ballet.

Move! Pleasure wanted to shout at them, but there was no point; no possibility of hurrying them. Their clothes hung like wind-abandoned banners. Their fingers hovered indecisively, one moment packing, the next moment retreating into the meditative world of slow all-over scratching which allayed the heroin itch. The two mobile ones were again ready to fix. Still shivering, the third had gathered himself into a hunched-up sitting position from which he looked out at the world with complete disinterest.

He raised his eyes to Pleasure, an opaque stare cauterized of all emotion. Looking back into those pale-blue, burnt-out pupils, Pleasure found no contact. There was only a void into which he felt himself falling.

'The water,' the boy told him, his voice flat as his stare.

'Water?'

'Yeah, I fixed the water, man.'

'What water?' Pleasure asked.

'Cistern . . . ' the kid waved a backhanded disclaimer of responsibility. 'Some cat left the top off,' he told Pleasure. 'See?'

Pleasure nodded and looked away. He could still feel the junkie's stare. He crossed to the other door and down the passage to the bathroom. The lid was still off the cistern – parked on the floor where Patrick had left it. As he pissed, Pleasure looked down into the tank. The water was rust-tainted and faintly stained with mud.

Easier to dip a spoon into the open cistern than turn a tap? Pleasure shrugged. Either way the water had to be lousy with bacteria. Houseboats pumping sewage into the lake. Steady seepage from the city. The inside of his arm seemed to swell out naked and unprotected. The image of a needle digging and hunting for a vein jerked him forwards retching into the toilet pan. Head supported on his hands, he knelt trembling on the cold linoleum.

'They've gone.'

Pleasure looked up.

Patrick stood propped in the doorway. The alcohol had puffed the skin below his eyes. Their definition lost, the whites had become a muddy no-man's-land. His mouth slumped.

'You look like hell,' Pleasure told him.

'Wipe your mouth.'

Pleasure spat. 'I'm going to wash,' he said as he flushed the toilet. He brushed his teeth, rinsed his mouth.

'So?' he asked.

Silence.

Pleasure picked up his comb. As he did his hair, his eyes skittered across the mirror in search of an angle from which to watch his companion.

'So?' he asked again.

He risked a quick glance into the reflection of Patrick's eyes.. There was a moment of contact – then Pleasure was back to arranging his hair and Patrick to brooding contemplation of the floor. The silence was ridiculous.

'Shit!' Pleasure swore. 'Look at us. We're like a couple of fucking fairies.' He spoke to the mirror. 'Go on,' he demanded, 'look at us! Me with my hair, you sulking in the doorway. Two queens on a houseboat. Married bliss! How long are we going to keep this up?'

'You started it,' Patrick countered.

'I?' Pleasure snapped. 'What about you and your junkie friends? *Mr Cool* stoned-out drunk – table burnt. Some crazy smackhead ODing on the goddam couch and the music so loud every cop in Kashmir must have heard it.'

'So what are you frightened of?' Patrick demanded. He looked up finally, angrily. 'Georgia cracker,' he told Pleasure. 'That's you. So paranoid and prejudiced there's no point in even talking.'

'Prejudiced!' Pleasure retorted. 'Who's the narco? Who gets paid for persecuting them?'

'Who pays the rent!' Patrick shouted.

'Not you!' Pleasure jerked round to face the Irishman. 'Not you and that's for sure.'

'My damn salary.'

'Paid from taxes.'

'You pay taxes?' Patrick demanded.

They stood glowering at each other across the yellow linoleum floor of the small bathroom. Out of the silence a night owl hooted gently from over the other side of the bridge. Almost a croon, that bird cry, crop full, a croon of soft contentment which drew Patrick's eyes away from the challenge. He looked towards the window. Black night. He wanted to sleep, to surrender to the weight of the rum; but there was still an Irish stubbornness which refused him abdication.

'He had hepatitis,' he said. 'The kid on the couch.'

'So he shoots piss in his veins, I'm meant to care?' Pleasure asked.

'He's sick,' Patrick insisted. 'They wanted a bed for one night.'

'Sick!' Pleasure exploded. 'What are you? Medicare? You're a fucking narco, not the Public Health Department. We can't run a hospital.' He shrugged helplessly. 'I mean, don't you know about junkies?'

But Patrick didn't. Or not the way Pleasure meant. Not even junkies stole from the Justice Department. They saved that act for their friends, family and benefactors. Three bankrupt heroin addicts! Even in India that meant five dollars a head per diem – and that just to keep them out of pain. Fifteen dollars a day to be begged, borrowed or stolen . . . and then the police coming round; searching; asking questions. Only the rich could afford addicts or addiction.

'We don't have the bread,' he told Patrick. 'Don't you see?' he insisted. His thoughts had moved to the pile of receipts and tickets he'd still to manipulate into last month's expense account.

'There's two of us already,' he said . . . and, suddenly sad for Patrick, 'I'm sorry about the rum.'

'You shouldn't have left me alone,' Patrick told him. His eyes fled round the small bathroom. 'It's like a jail.'

'This? You have to be joking!'

Patrick managed a smile. 'You're the specialist,' he admitted.

Pleasure grinned. 'Too right,' he said. He turned to replace his comb on the shelf above the basin. Watched Patrick's reflection. 'I've scored,' he stated flatly. 'The dope's on the boat.'

Patrick crossed to the window, pushing it open to air out the sour stench of vomit. The owl hooted again.

'You want to bust me, now's your chance.'

Patrick shivered. 'Jesus it's cold.'

'That's an answer?'

'*Man,* but you nag.' Closing the window, the Irishman

turned to look at his companion. 'It's like that dog,' he said. 'You're not much but you're all I've got.'

CHAPTER THREE

The Air India flight landed at Panjim Airport, Goa. Patrick and Pleasure took the airline bus into Panjim then a cab out to Calangute beach. The narrow, tarred road threaded its way between plantations of coconut palms, emerald-bright paddy fields, and gently decaying villages, half deserted.

Licensed to smuggle freely into the subcontinent, Portuguese Goa had been rich if venal. Indian Goa was a corrupt dead-end – a cul-de-sac of dying memories.

The cab, a ten-year-old British Austin, stopped outside the post office in Calangute village. A moment later Patrick found himself being dragged with their bags into the back of an open Land Rover packed with Pleasure's friends.

His face squashed into two brown thighs, the Irishman gasped for breath as the Rover lurched forward out of the village towards the sea. He had the image of a dark Goan rushing out of a tailor's kiosk to grab Pleasure's hand as they passed; a restaurant, a dozen windowless shops with double doors wide open, a small market with corrugated iron roof supported on stubby pillars, a cab rank.

The driver hooted incessantly. A tape recorder blared out an album from the Grateful Dead and a large ivory chillum got thrust down at his face. As Patrick shook his head, his lips involuntarily brushed the smooth inner skin of the thighs which held him pressed with his back against their baggage. The bikini-clad owner of the thighs whistled. Tugging his head back, Patrick looked up over sunburnt belly and breasts into deep brown laughing eyes.

'Hi,' the girl said, 'I'm Judy. Who are you?'

'Patrick,' Patrick told her and took off his tie for something to do with his hands.

The Land Rover turned off the tar on to a bumpy track leading directly to the beach. The tyres hit a rut. The girl lost her footing. Collapsed on to Patrick's lap. The Rover stopped. Someone silenced the tape.

'So now we've met,' Judy said with a wide warm grin, as Patrick struggled to help her up.

Eleven of them got down from the truck. There was Texas Tom, he owned the Land Rover; Pleasure and Blind Nick; Tom's Sandy, eight months pregnant, and German Susie – she with long blonde hair right down to her ass: these from the front. Tom had been driving.

From the back came Judy, who was Chicago Jewish, Black Jack, Frank'n'Ellen, whose names got slurred together because that's the way the couple was, Patrick, and a blonde Swiss girl who'd flagged Tom for a ride. No one knew the Swiss girl. Bar Patrick, the rest were close family. Ibiza family. They summered together, wintered together, and those that needed the bread ran hash together. But for this last, they were much like any other favoured leisure group . . . except they spent less and never drank enough to get drunk. For Pleasure this was the first time he'd felt truly joyous since the police chief had warned him off.

Rammed up by centuries of monsoon surf, the final fifty yards of land before the beach formed a ridge which sloped gently back towards the road in one direction and steeply down to the sea in the other. Along the seaward edge of this ridge, storm winds had thinned the coconut palms, and those left standing were bent and swayed like the wrinkled trunks of buried mammoths.

The house Black Jack had found for Pleasure this season stood amongst these trees. It was a fisherman's house: small, white-walled, tile-roofed, with the roof extending forward towards the sea to form a shady terrace on which swung a hammock and a kerosene lamp. The front door stood open as were both windows.

Five people waited on the terrace – more of the family; French Pierre the photographer with his wife Jeanette, Pierre's younger brother Titi, Arabella, who was British – she was Titi's girl and lay with her head on his lap – and Garments Gerry, who was New York and a non-kissing cousin, in fact a drag. He had the hammock.

All five lazing on the terrace wore thin silver belts over which were looped narrows strips of cotton drawn loosely up between their thighs. They were smoking an Arabian water pipe.

Shy of the welcoming commotion on the terrace, Patrick waited by the Rover. Below him lay the sea – a blue plane of shimmering light reflections bordered by eight hundred yards of pale gold sand which curved gently round to end against the foot of a high bluff of dark-red coral. On the naked peak of this point, he could see the ruins of a church outlined against the sky, while directly below where he stood lay four large outrigger canoes in the shade of which squatted half a dozen Goan fishermen mending their nets.

'Satisfied?'

Startled, Patrick spun round. Judy stood there. Smiling at him. He nodded.

'Did I mess your clothes?'

He looked down at himself. Black shoes, White shirt. Dark-blue suit. Sand lapped his carefully polished toecaps. Her feet, naked, a chip off the corner of one nail . . . and a thin inch-long scar curving round from her right shin.

Tie dangling from his left hand, he glanced up. Their eyes met. He smiled sheepishly. Looked beyond her to the house. Pleasure stood laughing on the terrace beside a young Goan girl who held a broom. Gazing up at the American in obvious adoration, the Goan girl balanced on one foot while she rubbed the back of her calf with the other. Patrick knew she was blushing.

'Come look,' Pleasure shouted.

The Irishman nodded. He felt out of place. 'I'm not dressed right,' he said.

'True,' Judy agreed.

He wanted to touch her – to put his arm round her

124

shoulders; that casual gesture which came naturally to Pleasure and his friends. She waited.

Then, 'See you later,' she said quietly and ran off down the beach to the sea.

Patrick turned to join the others.

Their house consisted of a front room opening to the terrace with, left and right, two small bedrooms. Kitchen, bath, and a large store previously used for stacking nets were at the rear with the privy ten yards behind the back entrance. The kitchen and left-hand bedroom opened off the living-room, with the bath connected to the kitchen by a doorway with no door. The only entrance to the store and second bedroom was from outside the house. There was no electricity and water came from a well.

Furniture consisted of a cotton-stuffed mattress in each bedroom and four more of these in the front room plus a table. Plates, glasses, cutlery, five cooking pots and a kettle were arranged on a stone shelf in the kitchen. The stove was two small charcoal braziers. All these possessions were Pleasure's. He had left them for the Goan girl to store.

'Would you believe it?' he demanded delightedly. 'Nearly three years!' He turned to the girl. 'Antoinette, this is Patrick.'

Patrick took the small brown hand. He guessed she was sixteen – seventeen at the most. She was very shy.

'Welcome,' she whispered.

'Thank you.'

'She'll clean for us,' Pleasure explained. 'Which room do you want?'

Patrick chose the right-hand one for the extra privacy of its own front door. 'I'd better change,' he said.

Black Jack's ivory chillum lit and circulating, they lay drying on the beach. The family. They were all there except for Judy and Garments Gerry. The shade of a canoe protected their heads while the talk drifted lazily as summer clouds. Ibiza talk. Family talk.

'And you?' Jack asked into a pause.

Pleasure reached for the chillum. He'd already told them how he'd got ripped off in Istanbul. 'I'd like to try the islands,' he said. 'Bali first, then the South Pacific.' He took a drag at the pipe, rolled over and sat up.

Patrick watched him.

Pleasure gave the Irishman a smile. 'I'll have to get a number together first,' he said. 'How much bread do I have?'

'Seven fifty,' Jack told him. He'd sold Pleasure's sound equipment as well as his bike.

Pleasure calculated. It was not enough. The way prices were in India he'd need over seven hundred dollars for six kilos of Bombay Black plus another five hundred for air fares and expenses – then there were the two hundred dollars he owed Patrick for the Kashmiri Black he'd bought, plus fifty for the carpet he'd presented to the farmer in return for the Pahelgham. He'd need to earn some bread.

Still watching Patrick, 'Anyone want cases made?' he asked and passed the chillum.

Susie took it. 'Garments,' she suggested. 'He's got two kids at his place he's priming to run.'

Pleasure grimaced.

'You asked,' she said and turned to face the Irishman. 'You in on this?'

Pleasure grinned at his companion. Winked.

'In a way,' Patrick admitted. They talked about dope runs the way most people discussed going to the bank, he thought, as he shook his head at the proffered chillum. The only one in swimming shorts, he still felt overdressed. And he wanted a drink.

Leaving unobtrusively, he first swam then strolled slowly on down the beach with his feet in the shallow ripples where shells lay turned by the tide. He wondered where Judy was – or who she was with.

He passed half a dozen groups of young Westerners lying out on the sand. They all looked up as he passed; smiled, waved. There was something that looked like a bar down the far end of the beach. He'd get himself a drink, he decided, then walk into the village to buy a couple of those cotton strips the others wore intead of shorts. And maybe a silver belt.

Lying in the back of Tom's Land Rover that evening, Pleasure felt he weighed no more than two pounds. They were on their way over to Anjouna, the next beach up the coast. This was where Garments Gerry had a house. The trip was Jack's idea.

'Get the work booked,' he'd said. 'Then you can relax.'

Two hundred dollars for a good false bottom was the going rate ... though right now Pleasure could not be bothered thinking about bread. They'd smoked good dope all afternoon as well as eating hash cookies Tom's Sandy had brought down to the canoe. Now he felt so light he knew one strong gust of wind would float him right out of the truck. He laughed.

'Hold me down,' he begged Susie. He lay flat on his back with his head in her lap. She too started to laugh, as did Black Jack who'd been struggling to fill his chillum.

'Man, I can't get this together,' Jack complained. He stuffed his pipe back in the pouch he wore on his belt and kept on laughing while up front the stocky black-haired Texan rapped out a tattoo on the horn.

'Let's get it on,' Tom shouted. 'Let's get it onnnnnn!' That last word drawn out and out till the palms shivered overhead, a green tunnel or arched latticework down which they drove for what seemed like eternity with the horn going *pup-p-pup paaap* and Tom bellowing his war-cry again and again.

Now everyone was laughing. Tears blinding him, Pleasure rolled his head in Susie's lap for the joy of feeling her through the thin silk sarong.

'Tom!' he shouted. 'We have it on.'

'Right on!' This from Jack. And so they reached Anjouna beach.

Typical of Garments, Pleasure thought, as he looked up the mouldering mansion the New Yorker had rented. Garments had to have the biggest. That was his trip. One more Danish Pete.

'I don't think I can make that scene,' he murmured up at

Susie. 'Not yet. You want to swim?'

A steep coral bank overhung the beach. They clambered down to walk hand in hand round the next point to a small cove. It was almost dark. Naked, they raced into the sea. Fluorescent spray curled round their legs. The first stars were clear overhead while up on the cliff the palm trees leant in towards each other, stirring softly, kissing.

Susie floated on her back. Arms extended, her hands paddled gently, balancing her body against the swell. Pleasure dived, rolled underwater, looked up at her outline. Minute bubbles powdered her flanks with diamonds. Her long hair drifted free, a soft cloud of flowing iridescence. His hands trickled up the channel of her spine, played in her hair, grabbed for the stars. He spouted salt, gulped air, somersaulted, swam to the sea floor, plucked a shell, surfaced again. The air rushed into his lungs. He rolled lazily along her thigh. Placed the petal of pearl in the curl of her navel.

Susie lifted his offering to her mouth. Her tongue slid over the shell's smoothness. Pink tongue. Eyes dreaming. Mind free. Body languorously open as if it were a flower unfurled to the moon. Swell-rocked, drifting shoreward. Kneeling on the sand with the warm sea breeze breathing over their bodies. The wet cloak of her hair. Her sarong spread. Her teeth and the whites of her eyes bright lights in the tan of her face. Waves rolling lazily on to the sand . . . sea rhythm of which they were a part so that Pleasure moved with the surf, washed forward, slow withdrawal, then washed in again on another swell . . . and no sense of each other nor of themselves – but only this slow joyous flowing in which they were melted into the sea and the stars and the softly whispering palms.

Patrick had a successful afternoon. He discovered two locally brewed spirits, one distilled from cashew and the other from palm juice. The cashew fenny was a disaster. One sip and he remembered from childhood a big can of detergent cream kept by the tap in the back of the machine shop round the corner from his parents' apartment.

Fortunately the palm fenny was delicious, especially when drunk iced and with fresh lime. He bought two bottles for the equivalent of an American quarter, the shop owner filling the bottles from a drum. He also purchased a bag of fresh limes, an ice bucket filled with cubes from the store's ancient Kelvinator, a manual juice extractor and a jug. All these he brought home together with a silver belt and two of the cotton strips which everyone wore on the beach.

Now, with a drink mixed and ready beside him on the terrace, he lay gently swinging in the hammock. He hadn't eaten but was not particularly hungry. Nor was he lonely – or not more so than he was used to.

Pleasure had left a note pinned to the door so Patrick knew where they'd gone and could follow if he so desired. He didn't. From the hammock he could see three other houses. The closest was Judy's. *We've gone,* Pleasure had written and there was no lamp lit in Judy's house.

Sipping his drink, Patrick lay listening to the slow churn of the sea. From the far end of the beach by the bluff drifted voices softly chanting to the beat of drums.

The ice tinkled against the side of his glass and Patrick smiled contentedly. How long could this last, he wondered. He had not meant this doubt to creep so insidiously into the calm. He fought back ... no longer sipping now, but gulping, and then carrying his empty glass directly back into the kitchen.

He drained the newly made drink while standing by the stove. It did not help. He walked, almost ran, down to the sea. Barefoot, he wore a pair of Pleasure's jeans and a white shirt. The drums gave him a temporary goal. He walked slowly as if to extend this safety of direction. The waves played with his feet, throwing curls of foam over his insteps and through his toes; foam flecked with phosphorescence and the stars immensely clear.

A bonfire spouted sparks below the cliff. Approaching, Patrick saw the outline of small figures squatting round the flames. Brown faces and arms dyed red by the flames, the fisher families swayed to the beat dictated by two musicians who each held two drums clamped between their legs. The rhythm was slow. The circle swayed gently, the chant rising and falling in time with the drums and sea ... they the water, Patrick guessed, while the drums were the boats and paddles dipping.

For an hour he stood watching and listening till slowly the circle broke. The drummers smiled calmly as they wiped their foreheads free of sweat. Soft partings whispered, the chanters drifted homewards. Patrick turned reluctantly. Low above the trees hung four stars forming a cross. He had no wish for reminders of the Church, the Passion ... yet the reminder existed there in the sky so that he found himself praying for the first time in years. Not true prayer, but silent incantation ... 'The Lord is with thee, blessed is the fruit of thy womb, Jesus. Holy Mary Mother of God pray for us sinners now and at the hour of our death.' Again and again these words ran through his mind like a cleaning cassette played through a dusty recorder. And the act of contrition as he neared the house: 'Forgive me my sins, oh Lord ... ' but then he heard a noise from within the front room.

'Pleasure?' he called as he reached the terrace. No answer. The front door stood open as they'd agreed – valuables to be kept locked in their bedrooms. A cat in the kitchen, he wondered. He reached the door. A dark shape rushed. He responded from the training manual – no thought. A brief cry silenced by his left hand. Then he remembered himself.

Removing his hand from the girl's mouth, he swung her round by the wrist he'd caught up behind her back so that now she faced him. She was painfully thin: Caucasian, he catalogued; blonde, age 23, height 5ft. 3in., weight 85 to 90 – he couldn't see the colour of her eyes. Her arms gave her away. Dark-blue track marks. Collapsed veins. Ulcer scars.

'Who are you?' he asked, then shrugged because it did not matter who she was. He could feel her trembling and her body was hot and wet with sweat. He guessed she was at least twelve hours overdue.

'Can you score on the beach?' he asked.

She nodded.

'Now?'

Again she nodded.

He took out his wallet before letting go her wrist. 'How much?'

There came a moment's hesitation while she tried to gauge how large a touch he'd stand.

'Don't lie,' he told her quietly.

'Five . . . ?' she tried.

'Rupees?'

She nodded.

'And five for the morning?'

Again that quick nod . . . as if she were scared to speak, he thought. He held his wallet up to the kerosene lamp. He searched quickly. Found a ten.

She took the bill as if it were the baton in a relay race. Her thanks came over her shoulder as she dashed off through the trees.

'See you around,' he called. Poor chick – she must be feeling like a man bursting to piss who makes the loo only to find the door locked; but a thousand times worse, Patrick thought, as he walked through to the kitchen. He had a quick drink while squeezing fresh lime into the jug. The second he carried out to the terrace.

Judy sat on the steps.

'Hi,' he greeted her. 'I thought you went to Anjouna.'

'To see Garments?' Her grin registered disbelief. 'I've seen him already this year.'

'That bad?'

She laughed as she nodded. 'Pretty bad.'

Patrick sat down on the same step. 'Why Garments?' he asked.

'He used to sell bras.'

'So you're snobs?'

'I guess,' Judy admitted, ' . . . or maybe it's Gerry.' She smiled. 'You'll see.'

'That a threat?' he asked and handed her his drink to try. He watched her mouth as she sipped. Her bottom lip protruded slightly – a wide, generous mouth with strong white teeth.

'Ice!' she exclaimed delightedly. Her eyes shone in the soft light of the lantern. 'Hey, you're not so lost.'

'Lost?'

'That's what I thought,' she told him. 'Remember when we picked you up. You looked lost – you in your suit and all those bags. What do you do?'

'Lost or out of place?'

'Lost,' she insisted and watched him fumble for a cigarette. 'Not for me.'

Patrick flicked his lighter, drew and puffed. 'If you're going to hold on to that drink,' he said, 'then I'd best mix myself another.'

She looked at him over the top of the glass. 'Wait while I finish,' she told him. Sipped and went on watching him. 'That gives you time to answer my question and you'll save yourself a trip.'

'Question?'

'What do you do?'

'Nothing.' he smiled. 'Except drink,' he said. Her eyes went serious.

'I'm sorry,' he said. 'I'm meant to work in an office. Maybe I've quit. Before that I was in Vietnam and before that at graduate school. Cornell,' he added. 'I didn't finish.'

Now it was her turn to smile. Swallowing the rest of the fenny, she handed him the glass. 'Don't shit me,' she told him. *Never*. Right?'

He nodded. 'I'll get those drinks.'

Incense sticks glowed on the stairs up to the living-room in Garments Gerry's house. The room was large and high ceilinged. Kutch embroidery decorated the walls; Hindu prints, temple hangings. A tray on his lap, the New Yorker sat cross-legged on a low dais spread with cushions. Razor blade in hand, he glanced up as Pleasure and Susie entered.

'Hi,' he greeted them and went back to knifing cocaine on to a playing card, cutting the white crystals into fine powder ready for snorting. Two late-teenage to early-twenties Canadian girls knelt watching him – as if he were some sort of god, Pleasure thought.

Swimming with Susie and then making love on the beach had brought him down from that first high peak he'd reached in the Land Rover. Now the hash he'd eaten came sweeping in again. He found a pillow over by the back wall where Jack lolled with the soles of his narrow black feet showing pale, milk chocolate in the candlelight.

'Those the runners?' Pleasure murmured.

'Right,' Jack told him.

'They don't look like they're even weaned,' Pleasure complained, as he listened to Garments lay his drug ostentation rap on the two young Canadians. Clip, clip went the razor blade while the New Yorker trotted out the list of herbs and chemicals he'd taken as if he were a peacock and the drugs his fan: daturi root from Bengal, psylocibin mushrooms plucked in the Bali rain forests, peyote from Mexico, opium and all its distillates, mescaline – and then that array of capital letters which lengthened every year: DET, DPT, LSD, STP, THC, DMT, MDA ... a whole crazy alphabet to fuck your mind, Pleasure mused, as he half floated there against the wall. It was the same old Cadillac game, he decided, as he watched and listened. Status symbols. But then that was Garments' trip.

Tom was over there stoned-out in a rocking chair. His thatch of black hair tumbled over his forehead so that he looked like a shaggy Shetland pony. Head cocked, he sat listening with his mouth half open in gentle amazement. Every few minutes he'd slowly shake his head, That was the most he could manage. And Sandy was asleep. Sandy addicted to balling – how was she doing now, Pleasure wondered, as he inspected her swelling belly. She looked good pregnant: tanned and fertile, he thought and looked back at Garments.

The New Yorker had produced a fat wallet from which he took a note, rolled it into a narrow tube and snorted the first two lines of coke. A hundred-dollar bill, Pleasure guessed ... and was right.

'You want me to make those cases?' he asked.

Garments gave him a put-down grin. 'If you haven't lost your touch in jail.'

'Thanks,' Pleasure said. ' And that's two fifty a bag.'

'Hey!'

'Crap,' Pleasure told him. 'Find someone else or pay my price.'

'Right on!' Jack supported.

Pleasure stood up. 'And don't let him shit you,' he warned the Canadians. 'It's your risk and I'm the best.' He grinned. 'And fuck you,' he added, addressing Garments. 'You ever had the balls to make your own run?'

'Cool it,' Jack said, and Tom laughed.

'Let's split.'

Her back resting against a pillar of the terrace, Judy sat watching Patrick. They'd had two drinks each plus a shared bowl of rice and vegetables she'd fetched from her house.

'Tired?' she asked.

'A little.'

The way he answered sounded like an excuse, she thought. She could not place him. The family all looked younger than their age. Problem free. Open. Patrick, with those deep ravines flaring out from his nose, seemed somehow already old. Disappointed. And his eyes kept losing her. Shutters, she thought. And for a moment she wondered why she bothered. Then the shutters rose again. It was as if there were someone hiding in there, small and warm and defenceless . . . to which she felt all her maternal instincts suddenly respond so that she sat with her entire body melting into her loins and her hands almost uncontrollable. Yet if she moved, she knew he'd run. Like playing a fish, she thought suddenly remembering a childhood holiday spent in the Upper Peninsula. Trout fishing! Her father had been playing W A S P those years. Pride at the Six Day War had brought him back to being a Jew – not synagogue, just the upper-crust Israel Bond set. Which was not much to have dropped out from, she thought as she stretched leisurely, breasts thrusting forward, then stood up. She did not risk looking at Patrick.

'Come on,' she said. 'Let's swim before bed.'

'I'll fetch a towel,'

'Don't bother,' she told him.

They walked down to the water with a yard between them. Judy stopped by the first outrigger. Unfastening her sarong, she draped it over the prow of the canoe. There was no moon but the stars were so bright he could see her clearly. She stood with her back to him, deep tanned, long hair tumbling, shallow-shadowed spine, buttocks swelling, dark trench.

Shy of his erection, he waited fully dressed till she ran on into the sea. She was already a long way out by the time he followed. He did not try to catch her. Swimming was not one of the arts you learnt as a child on Avenue B. But Judy? He guessed her family was rich. There would have been pools at school and at the week-ends. Florida winters. The Bahamas.

Turning on his back, he lay floating. It ought to be easy to be happy, he thought ... and he remembered his prayers from earlier that evening. *Please make this work,* he whispered.

Her breathing still unhurried, Judy ghosted back to his side. He had not heard her coming. She was smooth as a seal, he thought, as he watched the water slide shinily over her dark skin.

Her hand brushed his – gently – perhaps by accident.

'Shall we go in?' she asked.

They took their clothes from the canoe. Patrick could feel his penis shrunk ridiculously small by the sea. He wanted to cover himself. But she did not look at him. Her hand slid into his. 'Is there water in the bathroom?' she asked.

Patrick didn't know. But there was. Antoinette had left three full buckets beside the tub. The poured one each over themselves.

'Towels in your room?'

Patrick nodded.

She held out her hand for the key. 'Will you mix the drinks?'

Patrick poured fenny over the last of the ice then stirred the juice of four limes into the glass. She hadn't come back. Almost reluctantly, he carried the drinks round the corner of the house. The door to his room was open. She knelt on the mattress drying her hair, a candle stood lighted on a brick beside the bed.

She looked up. 'You've never done that before — swum with a girl at night.' She wasn't asking. 'What did you do when you were young?'

'Lived in a slum,' he told her with a grin, putting lots of Irish into his voice.

'And at college?'

He shrugged. 'Worked.'

In fact that was all he'd ever done till he'd joined the army, he recalled now, as he looked down at her. There'd been little time for girls even if there'd been the money. He wasn't particularly clever. Hard slog, plus the drive of his mother's fantasies, had got him to school with a grant. Work had kept him there. Studying at home had been easy — the privacy his books granted him being infinitely preferable to either the violence of his brothers or the street. Cornell had been harder, but by then he'd already become so barricaded that he was left with few options.

He shook his head in rueful memory of the few clumsy attempts he'd made. 'No swimming,' he assured her. 'And no real chicks.'

'None?'

'Prostitutes,' he told her, his voice flat and his recollections of Tu Do Street in Saigon even more distasteful than they had been before: the pretence of love he'd gone through — the grimy *search* for love — and then the guilt and the fear as he'd tried to clean himself afterwards. That's all there had ever been. Whores and Scotch. He avoided her eyes as he took the towel from Judy.

'Don't do that!'

'What?' he asked. He was shocked by the sudden fierceness in her voice.

'Shut me out — don't ever do that.' Then she smiled again.

136

'And don't pretend you didn't,' she chided. 'You did.'

Grinning, he nodded sheepishly.

'Come here,' she commanded. Voice quiet, her hand patted the mattress. 'And you don't need that towel. You're dry.'

As he sat, she moved off the mattress to kneel at his feet. Arms out, her fingers touched his checks, drawing his eyes up to meet hers – semitic eyes – deep, sluggishly sensual umbras.

She leant forward. Part open, her lips brushed his mouth. Then she sank back on to her heels. Her thighs were broadened by the way she knelt: smooth, cinnamon-gold promontories protecting a silk-grown ravine. Her breasts swelled towards him. One satin curve glowed amber in the candlelight, the sharp shadow of the point leaping the valley to greet its twin.

He touched her nipples.

His hands were tentative. Curious. Like a child's, Judy thought, as she watched his fingertips trace tiny circles; watched her nipples stiffen ... and then suddenly that hollowness in her centre, that collapsing inwards ... as if her womb were a black hole in space. And for a moment she could not see. Then she smiled.

She drew away the protective towel from his loins. 'Lie down,' she whispered.

Her hair fell in a thick curtain which stroked gently over his body as she turned her face to his. For a moment he was frightened. Exposed and frightened. Then he felt his burgeoning strength. He tried not to think of how often his erections had died in the past. Those sweaty fumblings which had ended in failure and despair above the mocking black eyes of a small Vietnamese; failure made even more obvious and unbearable by his size – he a Westerner, tall, muscular, educated and impotent – impotent as the power and wealth he'd represented. *Too much drink*, he'd mutter – as if the girl had cared! But then the excuse had been for himself, not for her.

'What is it?' Judy asked. She felt him try to remain withdrawn within himself.

'Tell me,' she insisted.

His cheeks hot with embarrassment, "I'm not always too good at this,' he murmured.

'Why?' she asked.

Guilt, he almost said. But that was another excuse. 'Fear of failure . . . ' His voice drifted into silence.

Wait, she warned herself and fought down the temptation to take him in her arms. He looked so haggard, she thought. A cancer victim. Contagious cancer.

'You can't fail,' she told him, her voice deliberately light. 'Love's not a competition.'

His shoulders wrinkled the sheet as he shrugged. 'Maybe it just seems that way,' he said. He smiled wryly. 'The thirty-minute erection. That's part of the U.S. code of standards with Hugh Heffner as Bureau Chief.'

Smiling, she ran her fingers softly up the ridge of his swollen penis. 'Look,' she told him. She held it erect in her right hand. 'Does that seem like failure?' Her hair tricked over the tip. Her tongue touched it. A small pearl appeared.

For a moment she looked at him again. Into his eyes. Her lips were slightly parted. Wide lips, welcoming. And her eyes were sleepy dark with no white showing. Then her head bent over his loins and the black tent of her hair enclosed him.

CHAPTER FOUR

Patrick awoke with the warmth of the sun reaching halfway up his legs. Judy lay with her head on his chest, her right arm stretched across his body, her hand tucked into his armpit as if they belonged together. He had never woken like this before. He could not fully raise his head nor reach for a sheet without disturbing her. He looked down the length of her back and through the valley of her buttocks as if they were the open V of a rifle sight. The girl of the previous night squatted by the door. The junkie.

Seeing his eyes open, she waited for him to focus and be properly awake. He smiled.

'I made tea,' she said. Her voice was lightly accented – French, Patrick guessed – and she was younger than he'd thought. Not yet twenty. Her hair was cut short as a boy's, her eyes sunk deep in dark pits. She wore a man's shirt to cover her arms. A bamboo-patterned sarong cloaked the rest of her body except for her feet, which poked out, narrow, and all toes.

'There's no sugar,' she said.

Her voice woke Judy – or brought her out from the threshold of sleep. She raised her head, her cheek delicately lined with the patterns of his chest. She saw the girl. Smiling, she mumbled sleepily, 'Hi Marie,' before reaching for the top sheet which she pulled up to her waist. Only then did she look at Patrick. Lazy-eyed, she moved enough to kiss his throat before snuggling back down against his breast. Her eyes closed. Her breathing came slow and steady.

Patrick grinned. 'I'll have a job to drink,' he warned Marie as he watched her pour. 'You've breakfasted?'

She held up the cotton purse in which she kept her kit. Swung it gently. Her hypodermic clinked. She winked – a mischievous urchin, Patrick thought. Her teeth were still good,

139

so presumably she'd kept clear of shooting speed.

'And food?' he asked.

Her shrug came very French – ridiculously sophisticated considering how she looked. 'You hungry?'

'I'm human,' he told her. 'Here.' He found his cash. 'You want me trust you?'

She hesitated fractionally, grinned, and put her purse on the shelf by the door. 'Now I trust me,' she said and caught his wallet. 'What shall I get?'

'Enough for a couple of days,' he told her and laughed as the door closed. 'That's a good chick,' he said.

Judy raised her head. Chin supported in her hands, she looked down at him, surprise in her eyes – a trace of fear? 'You know junkies.'

'I know junkies,' he agreed.

Walking up the beach from the sea with the sun hot on his shoulders and already drying his hair, Pleasure felt fifteen and free. The joy was so full in him – so totally sensually full – that when he got to the top of the steep bank in front of the house he flung himself flat on the sand and rolled all the way back down again. He shouted as he rolled, the sky and the sea and the trees and the sand cartwheeling past his open eyes and his arms going thwack thwack as he spun. He ran back up to the house.

Antoinette skipped out of his way as he gained the terrace. She'd been watching him from the living-room while she swept. She always watched him. Broom in hand and laughing, she shooed him back to the sand. 'Wait,' she ordered. 'I fetch water.'

Under the trees to the left of the house a yoga class was in progress. The teacher was a young American, almost obscenely thin, and with long, lank hair. His back spattered by red spots with sunburst centres, he stood demonstrating a stomach-cleansing exercise to five equally young and thin disciples. Not pretty, Pleasure thought; they looked so joyless. Watching, he had not heard Antoinette return from the well.

'Yow!' he screeched as cold water cascaded over his head.

Laughing, he turned to face the second bucket. She threw him a towel and he saw the outline of her breasts as her bodice tightened. When he'd last been here she'd been a pretty child. Now she was beautiful. He wondered how she'd react to a pass ... an evil thought, he decided, and, shouting for Patrick, trotted through to the kitchen. Sight of Marie back from the village stopped him dead. Junkie! 'What in hell are you doing here?'

The French girl indicated the stove, her gesture curiously delicate.

'You've been here all night?'

She giggled at his surprise. 'Not all night,' she reassured. 'Short time. All night ten dollars. Short time two. You like?'

Right hand rumpling his hair, Pleasure grinned as he inspected the stove. 'I get any?'

'Two dollars, Mister.'

'How much for tea?'

'Free,' she told him. 'And there's toast.' She pointed to two covered plates. 'Knock,' she advised as an afterthought. 'Judy's with him.'

Judy the Jewish Mother! Perfect, Pleasure recognized. 'Tell them I'm over at Blind John's,' he said, and, grabbing two slices of toast, went out whistling.

Patrick sat in bed sipping tea and munching toast. The upper part of her body naked, Judy sat cross-legged beside him with the sheet lying loosely across her lap. Patrick was surprised at his easy acceptance of her casual nudity. His gaze drifted round the small room. His eyes came to rest on Marie. Home, he thought. That was all it took. If you had a reason for living then there was no need for junk. He watched the French girl pick nervously at her purse. She wanted to fix and he guessed she wanted to fix while they watched.

You could shoot for ten years and do little more harm to yourself than an alcoholic — though that was catastrophic enough! Equally you could shoot once and die. Heart failure, respiratory arrest: these were as much a part of an addict's life as were the lesser evils of blood-poisoning and hepatitis. If junk was your trip then you accepted the risks ... perhaps subconsciously desired them; though acceptance did not remove those last traces of natural fear. If you were going to die it was happier to have someone around to hold your hand. Patrick had seen too many needles to mind watching one more – he did not know about Judy.

Marie took the decision off his shoulders. She held up her purse and they heard the clink of glass. 'OK?' she asked Judy, who told her to go ahead.

They watched the French girl crush a morphine pill into a spoon. A second spoon she filled with water which she boiled briefly over the candle. Adding the morphine, she sucked the mixture up into a small syringe. The draw string of her purse she wound tight round her bicep and looked questioningly at Patrick.

Rocking forward on to his knees, the Irishman held the string taut while she searched for a vein. All he could see were dark tracks and the hollow troughs of flattened blood vessels.

Marie rubbed hard, flicked with her nail a couple of times, then dug deep. The needle hunted left and right till finally dark red oozed back into the hypodermic. With a smile of satisfaction she pushed the plunger home, nodded quickly, impatiently – and Patrick whipped the tie off fast.

'Wow,' she murmured and leant back against the wall as the rush swept her up.

Patrick took the syringe out of her hand. For the first few minutes she was cool; she just sat calmly smiling. Then she started to nod out. Her head kept falling forward on to her breast. If she'd kept that way – her head down and her eyes closed – then they could have ignored her. But she didn't. Every few minutes she'd temporarily recover. Her head would come slowly up. Eyes half-focused, her gaze would wander vacantly round the small room. Finally she would recognize them. For a moment a smile would lift her face; the smile of a small child drawn from her dreams. Then CRASH, and down would fall her head again.

Finally Patrick got out of bed. He wrapped Judy's sarong round his hips. 'I'll put her next door,' he said as he squatted down in front of the little junkie.

'Hey,' he whispered. He shook her gently by the shoulders. For a time nothing happened. At last her head came up. Slowly. She stared at him without apparent recognition. Then she giggled.

'C'est le gentil flic,' she murmured. She tried to raise her hand to stroke his cheek. The hand got only halfway.

'Gentil flic,' she whispered as he held her. She smiled sleepily. 'Je sais, je sais. Hier soir quand tu m'as piquée.' She tried to re-enact the way he'd grabbed her as she fled the living-room but her arms hardly moved. Her head fell forward. She'd nodded out again.

Patrick scooped her up in his arms. She weighed nothing. Carrying her round the house, he laid her gently in the corner of the main room where the breeze would keep her cool but where she'd be safely out from under foot.

Straightening up, he looked out of the window to the sea. He was surprised that, despite his desolation, he should feel for the girl such tenderness. His inclination was to run. Hide. Only hiding would not help. He went back to his room.

Judy sat waiting on his bed. The sheet was tucked up to her chin.

'She's all right,' he said.

Judy nodded. '*Flic* means cop,' she said. There didn't seem to be much of anything in her voice.

'That's right,' he said.

'Is that how you know about junkies?'

'Yes.' He thought of sitting down beside her but decided he was probably better off standing up. 'I work for Justice,' he explained quietly. 'Narcotics Bureau – Department of Narcotics and Dangerous Drugs.' He shrugged. 'At least I think I do.'

Then he sat down on the mattress anyway – the end of the mattress to give her room to get away. He had no idea what she thought. She looked much smaller than she really was –

perhaps that was the sheet.

'Mostly I'm in an office,' he continued. 'Frankfurt. I speak fluent German and some French. We had a case originating in Istanbul. I got sent there to check the records. Then they needed someone tailed. An emergency. There was no one else on tap and I'm the right age group.' He did not look at her.

'I'm following Pleasure,' he said.

'Does he know?' she asked. Her tone was abstract. Patrick felt as if he were eavesdropping on a conversation going on the other side of a partition wall.

'Oh, he knows,' he said. 'You see I'm not that hot at following and Pleasure didn't have any bread.'

She looked at him then.

'We get along pretty well,' he continued. 'That is except when I drink. I mean I don't get quarrelsome,' he assured her quickly, 'but you know – well I get pretty loaded, which sets Pleasure on to a kind of responsibility trip which really isn't his scene. Do you see?' he asked earnestly. 'What with my being bad at following and Pleasure having no bread, it just seemed sensible for us to get together. It was Pleasure's idea,' he added, as if that fact excused him . . . and he risked looking at Judy.

She tried not to laugh. Failed. 'You're mad,' she spluttered. 'Both of you – totally insane!' The sheet fell down to her lap. She sat there shaking her head in complete amazement. 'Totally, totally insane.'

Patrick grinned sheepishly. 'I don't know,' he protested, 'we thought we were pretty slick at the time.'

Patrick played Pleasure at chess down on the beach most of that afternoon. They sat with the board in the shade of a canoe while Judy lay sprawled in the sun.

The two men could almost be twins, she mused, as she watched Patrick prod a pawn forward one square. His gentle handling of Marie fitted no picture she'd ever had of how a narco would act. Back up at the house she'd asked him.

'You don't beat up on cancer patients,' had been his answer.

He'd glanced down at the night's empty glasses waiting to be washed.

'It's all escape,' he murmured. 'Your people watch TV?'

'Not so much.'

'Rich – maybe they didn't need to.' Irony more than anger or bitterness. 'Four hours nightly,' he told her from his memory of being a small child – falling – cracking his knee – wanting to weep – looking up at his mother, who sat solid as the Berlin Wall in front of a twenty-four-inch colour totem box ... no way through that wall nor point to weeping except inside himself.

'King Screen?' he asked Judy. 'Junk, booze – what's the difference?' Tidying their glasses on to the breakfast tray, he stood up and reached for her hand.

'Run baby, run,' he said. 'Maybe someday we'll outlaw what sets people running instead of what they use for fuel ... and maybe not,' he added. Pulled her to her feet. 'Want to make it down to the beach?'

Which was at least a beautiful escape, Judy thought now, as she lay with the heat forcing her down into the sand; forcing her down so hard she felt like bursting open. He had great legs, Patrick. Great legs and strong hands. Just lifting her ass would be good. Lying there the way she was and lifting her ass enough so he could slide in as if he were the sun. Her ass twitched involuntarily. Pleasure saw. Flicked a match.

She smiled lazily. Sex with Pleasure had been nice. A kind of relaxed incest was how she remembered him from the times they'd made it in Ibiza. Incest without guilt. And he was uncomplicated. Other men she'd balled got into weird gymnastics which was great till you realized they were working at it more than having fun. Men she could feel notching up her orgasms the way her father watched the ticker tape. Garments Gerry would be like that – not that she'd try – Wall Street Kamikaze on a ten-foot water bed. All give on the surface. Then you looked a little deeper and found it was all take. Chicks too, she thought, as she watched Pleasure frowning over his next move. She guessed Patrick had him trapped. Maybe even

145

herself the way she was always giving head . . . as with Patrick the previous night. Sucking him was sure to get him off. No risk – but to who's confidence? Pleasure had still not moved. Cheek on her folded arms, she closed her eyes.

'That's four you've won,' she heard Pleasure say.

Patrick smiled. He enjoyed playing Pleasure. Pleasure never minded losing. It was a drag having to watch an opponent get angry unless you were prepared to throw the game away.

'Swim?' he suggested.

Fifty yards out from the beach he turned on to his back. 'She knows,' he said.

'Judy?'

'Unhuh.'

'You tell her?' Pleasure asked.

'Marie guessed.' Patrick recounted how he'd caught the French girl trying to rob their house. 'Second nature,' he apologized.

'Both of you,' Pleasure agreed. 'Time you went back.' Spotting a cowrie, he dived before Patrick had time to answer.

The Irishman trod water, waiting. 'Why?' he asked when Pleasure surfaced.

Pleasure tossed him the shell. 'That or lose your job.'

Red with black markings, the cowrie glowed in the strong sunlight – like a ladybird, Patrick thought . . . *Fly Away Home.* He could see Judy sprawled dozing on a towel. 'Fuck my job,' he said. 'We can write a report that'll hold them till Christmas.'

'We!' Pleasure snorted and swam for the shore.

Patrick followed slowly. Too contented to worry, he walked up to the canoe to stand dripping straddle-legged over Judy.

Laughing, she rolled over. 'Pig!' she told him. 'You want to go up to the house?'

Patrick reached her down a hand.

'And that report?' Pleasure shouted after them.

Patrick waved.

At his door, Judy kissed him. 'I won't be long,' she promised. He watched her run off to her own house.

Leaving his door unlocked, he went round to the kitchen.

Squeezed a pitcher of lime. Judy was back by the time he'd finished. She'd brought a mirror, sarongs, towels, and a big red-and-white striped toilet-bag.

Throwing himself down on the mattress, he watched her arrange her possessions on the shelf by the door. He felt good – better than he'd ever felt in his life. 'Do you see your family?' he asked.

For a moment she looked surprised. Then she laughed. 'Of course.' She pushed the door half closed before slipping off her bikini to lie down beside him.

'Nice?' he asked.

'My family?'

He nodded.

Thinking of her two brothers more than her parents, 'Yes, they're pretty nice,' she said. They were a lot older though. By the time she'd been born they were already well into their own trips. Her mother too, so she'd gone young to kindergarten and from then on it had all been school and summer camp.

'I guess I was an accident,' she admitted. Rolling over, she ran her tongue up Patrick's ribs and into his armpit till he laughed with the tickling and wrestled her over on to her back.

'Tell,' he commanded.

He had a nice mouth, she thought. A nice mouth and lovely eyes containing always that trace of sadness which excited her.

'There's not much to tell,' she said. 'They're very generous and I had a good time – it was just that I was pleased to get out.'

'Why?' he insisted. She looked away. He waited.

It was mostly their wealth, she thought out loud ... their wealth and she being so much younger and a giver by nature. Money was hard to compete with. Fitting in had been about all she'd found to offer.

'I was always into their trips,' she told Patrick. 'Four of them so I was getting to be a four-way schizoid! But I love them,' she added seriously. 'Really – and it's good to know they're there.' She grinned. 'You know? If something went wrong. Which it hasn't,' she said.

'Touch wood,' Patrick warned and she knocked her knuckles gently against his skull.

CHAPTER FIVE

One week on Calangute Beach. Nothing had happened, Pleasure thought. Or nothing of moment. Two German kids on acid had jumped down a well in each others' arms. They had no idea why. Now both had broken legs.

A Dutch crazy had announced to the whole beach how he could walk on fire. Said he'd learnt in Bali. He'd dug a long pit which he'd lined with stones and charcoal. The flames had looked great at night. Either he'd been an inept pupil or only taken the beginner's course. Tom dropped him at the hospital before buying a large kingfish which they'd barbecued. The Dutchman would be out of bed for Christmas. They'd taken him a basket of fruit and some hash in thanks for the pit.

Jacques, a young French musician studying sitar at Benares University, had arrived for the vacation. He played for them most evenings.

Black Jack and a girl from Wyoming called Jane were going as steady as anyone had ever seen Jack go. He, Pleasure and Patrick had been out fishing with the Goans and were due to go again, and Garments had finally agreed to Pleasure's price for the bags so there were no money problems either.

The drag was Josephine. A twenty-eight-year-old French bitch, she'd brought four thousand morphine pills down from Bombay. She had a junkie chick from Queens called Roma blackmailed into making a run through to Kennedy once she'd found someone to make the cases. She'd asked Pleasure, which had got him so mad he'd tried bullying Patrick into writing a report. The Irishman had shrugged and said there was no point.

In fact, Patrick saw no point in anything except his present happiness – not even booze, which was nice to see, Pleasure admitted, but solved no problems.

The beach was at its most interesting around breakfast time, he decided. He had already swum. Now he sat on the terrace steps with a towel over his shoulders. Patrick sat beside him. Judy was in the kitchen with Antoinette.

The path down past their house bore a steady traffic of morning bathers. Pleasure had been counting with the aid of Patrick's watch and he reckoned the average at one swimmer every three minutes.

He was not convinced that any of this pre-breakfast mathematics meant much but what had started him calculating was the thought that, left to themselves, no one moved at the same speed with the result that the beach was never crowded.

He was about to point this out to Patrick when someone screamed the Irishman's name – a chick in panic. Patrick was up off the steps and sprinting before whoever it was could get his name out the second time. Pleasure ran after him.

Marie stood outside the third house back. Her mouth wide open, the cords on her neck stood out like strings on a double bass. Patrick charged straight in through the open door. A girl lay on the floor. Roma. Rigid. And her face was blue.

Throwing himself down beside her, Patrick forced open her mouth and dug her tongue out of her throat.

'Grab it,' he ordered as Pleasure joined him. Then he was astride her with his hands pumping air back into her lungs.

'Marie!' he bellowed, but the French chick was too shocked and doped out to help.

Judy came at a run. 'My medicine box,' Patrick told her. 'Quick!'

He glanced up at Pleasure – saw the anxiety. Shrugged as he pumped. 'Stupid bitch!'

Judy raced back in with his box.

'Open it,' he told her. 'Bottom right-hand corner – packet of long-needled syrettes marked adrenalin, a bottle of alcohol and a swab.'

Ripping the girl's sarong open he ran his fingers up over her heart. He found the gap between her ribs, grabbed the swab Judy passed, cleaned the mark just to the right of her breast, took the syrette out of Judy's right hand, paused one second – long enough to think *God, please* and to see Pleasure flinch with horror at the sight of the four-inch-long needle. Then he slid it firmly in and squeezed the syrette empty while slowly counting to five.

He reached for a fresh swab and plaster as he slipped the needle out. Giving her the empty syrette, he fixed the swab in place before continuing artificial respiration. The blue had gone out of her face and the rigidity had collapsed but he went on pumping for a few minutes more to be safe.

Her eyelids flickered. Taking her wrist, he timed her pulse against the second sweep on his watch. Looking up at Judy, he smiled. 'We going to get any breakfast this morning?' he asked.

'What do we do with her?' This from Pleasure, who still knelt by Roma's head.

Patrick shrugged. 'What do you want us to do?' he asked. 'She'll be conscious soon and she won't remember a goddam thing.' He looked down at her. 'That's the beauty of junk,' he said, 'an OD is as fast as Pentothol.'

Standing up with his medicine box in his right hand, he looked round for Marie. 'I don't suppose either of them even know how much she shot,' he said.

Squashed up in the far corner of the room, Marie resembled a shrunken famine victim. Glaring at her, 'You stupid bitch,' Patrick snapped. But that did no good.

He walked over and ran his hand gently through her cropped hair. 'Tell Roma to cut her dose in half,' he ordered. 'Can you remember that?'

Marie nodded. Tears trickled down her cheeks.

'Crying won't do any good,' he told her. 'If you want to die you want to die.' He walked out.

Antoinette had their breakfast ready on the terrace, but they had no appetite. Patrick accepted a cup of tea. His hands trembled. He needed to use his body – to reassure himself or cleanse himself from the proximity of death.

'You want to walk?' he asked.

'I can't,' Pleasure said. 'Garments said he'd bring the bread for the bags.'

'Bombay?' Patrick queried.

'Right,' Pleasure told him. 'I've a ride if he gets here before ten.' He watched Judy walk round to Patrick's room for her sandals. When she was out of earshot, 'That must have been Josephine's shit,' he said.

'Probably,' Patrick admitted.

'So?'

Patrick looked away.

'Well?' Pleasure insisted.

Still not looking at him, 'Let's talk about it when you get back,' Patrick said.

Which would mean one more cop-out, Pleasure knew, as he watched Patrick wander off with Judy through the trees. They walked hand in hand. Babes in the wood. Goddam junk, he thought. Junk was what screwed the whole beach scene.

He filled a fresh glass with tea and sweetened it with four heaped spoons of sugar, no milk. He carried the glass over to Roma's house. Marie had left her friend propped up against the wall in the sun. She looked bad but not too bad.

Pleasure squatted down beside her. Offered her the glass. Watched her sip.

'That Josephine's stuff you shot?' he asked.

'Right,' she murmured dreamily. She held the tea clutched in both hands but still looked like she might drop the glass so Pleasure took it back.

'Bombay?' he checked.

'Yeah,' she said. 'The Doc.'

Pleasure nodded. 'That's what I thought,' he said. 'Here.' He held the glass to her lips. 'Where's Marie?'

'Gone to the post.'

'Expecting bread?'

'We hope,' she answered. She looked up, a tentative smile hardly moving her lips. Her pupils were tiny islands in washed-out blue, her eye whites yellow from a messed-up liver. 'I guess I nearly bought it,' she whispered.

'Close,' Pleasure agreed. He gave her another sip of tea. 'I've got to get back,' he said. 'OK?'

Head against the wall, she closed her eyes. 'Great dream,' he heard her murmur to herself. Shit! he thought, and walked back to wait for Garments. An hour later he was on the road to Bombay.

Siesta hour. Pleasure lay on his bed in the Green Hotel. Arriving in Bombay at two o'clock that morning, he had slept till ten before completing his shopping. He could have caught the afternoon flight back south to Panjim but did not dare risk a search at Bombay's Santa Cruz airport. There was nothing illegal in the materials he would be carrying but they were certainly pointers to his intentions and travelling on a false passport made a careful document check as potentially dangerous as committing a crime.

Hijackers were a drag, he mused, as he swung his feet to the floor. When he'd first run dope, air travel had been a breeze. Now, with all the security measures in operation, it was getting to be a pain in the ass.

Pushing himself up off the bed, he walked over to the window. He'd been lucky to get a room at the Green. It was a cheap hotel but clean by Bombay standards, and looked out over Marine Drive to the sea.

Marine Drive is the Copacabana of the East; or that is its Bombay reputation. Pleasure had seen photographs of Rio. Standing here on the balcony, he had recollections of a blue sea, white sand and beautiful bodies. The water which lapped Marine Drive was dull milk chocolate, the patch of dun beach up the far end of the drive a public lavatory, and the few bodies visible at this moment looked half starved and probably were.

Goddam junk! Pleasure thought. Roma overdosing back on the beach had put him on a bum trip which he still could not shed. Suddenly angry, he turned back from the window, showered, dressed, and caught a cab down to the Taj Mahal

Hotel. Paying off the driver, he walked one block back from the sea front to the Rex.

Resembling four verandahed bungalows set one on top of each other, the Rex Hotel is headquarters for Western freaks in Bombay. Pleasure had stayed there often in the past. Now it attracted continual police surveillance so was to be avoided except from necessity. He waved to the manager as he entered. The front corner room on the top floor was his goal. He knocked. A tired voice bade him enter. Luigi lay on the bed.

As far as Pleasure knew, this tall, gaunt, long-haired Italian had lain on this same bed for the best part of seven years. Each morning he left for the opium den in Crawford Market at exactly nine forty-five. He stayed in the den two to three hours. Slept back at the Rex till eight in the evening, then returned to the den for his second session. Only twice had Pleasure seen him eat — both times at the Parsee-owned workmen's café on the corner before the Taj.

'Hi,' Pleasure greeted him.

Though they had not met for nearly three years, Luigi showed no surprise. Nothing surprised him any more — not even his opium dreams. He waved Pleasure to a seat on the bed. There was no other furniture. Two Western chicks lay sleeping on the patch of thin carpet which partly covered the floor. Naked but for knickers, they both lay curled up with their hands clasped between their thighs. One of them Pleasure remembered as American. The other he did not know. Addicts, he could see the outline of each bone. They had no breasts. Just nipples. He thought they looked like Belsen victims.

Nodding at them. 'The Doc still in business?' he asked.

Luigi nodded.

'Same address?'

Again that slow nod.

'Know the number?'

For a moment the Italian looked almost interested — but emotion was too much effort. Anyway Pleasure shook his head. 'Not for me,' he assured Luigi.

'Twenty-four,' the Italian told him. 'Second floor.' His

eyelids closed.

'Roma ODed on the beach,' Pleasure tried.

'Dead?' the Italian asked with his eyes still shut.

'We brought her round.'

Luigi did not even shrug. His voice had stayed the same right through and neither of the two junked-out chicks on the floor had stirred. A fly walked slowly across the face of the American girl. Pleasure watched the fly's progress. It reached the corner of her mouth. Squatted. Cleaned it legs. Flew to the light bulb. Pleasure looked back at the bed. Luigi slept.

'Thanks,' Pleasure said and left.

Five young heads in Hindi pyjama pants and no shirts sat circulating a chillum out on the landing. Pleasure passed a second group halfway down the stairs.

Street circus performers had erected a bamboo trapeze in the roadway while he'd been upstairs. A three-year-old girl lay blindfolded on the pavement waiting while her father strapped her to the end of a twenty-foot pole. Up the pole went, on to the man's forehead.

'You got five rupees?' an American voice panhandled from close by Pleasure's feet. He glanced down. Five freaks had camped against the parapet with a pipe passing back and forth. Beyond them an old woman squatted begging amongst the scurrying feet at the corner of the main road. Right hand out, her left touched her forehead in supplication. Almost naked, she was so old the muscles of her arms had melted into wrinkled sacks of skin hanging loose from the bone. Pleasure dropped fifty paise into her palm.

Runners for the black-market money-changers clamoured for his custom as he threaded the crowd. Escaping from these, Pleasure stumbled over a legless man in a clean white shirt. Set like an egg in an egg-cup, the man rested in a leather bowl nailed to a wooden tray that rolled on four brass castors. With a quick apology, Pleasure turned down a side-street and up the stairs of number twenty-four.

Twelve people waited in the Doctor's surgery. There were also two guards — thugs with weighted bamboo lathis bound with black insulation tape. They closed on Pleasure before he had both feet inside the door. He put as much warmth as he could into his smile. The guards were not impresssed.

'Doctor in?' he asked.

'Sit,' one of the toughs told him and gave him a shove.

Pleasure sat.

Four of the waiting patients were Indian. The rest were Westerners — two chicks, six males. All were young. None of them spoke. They sat with their eyes glued to the surgery door. One of the Indians, a boy who looked to be in his late teens, seemed more nervous than the rest.

Pleasure waited ten minutes before a male receptionist in a white coat came out of the doctor's office. Spotting Pleasure, his eyes flicked to the guards. All three advanced on the American.

'What do you want?' the receptionist asked. He had a quiet flat voice and his eyes held a look of permanent contempt.

Pleasure showed him a fifty-dollar bill. 'For a friend,' he said.

'Who sent you?'

'A Frenchwoman,' Pleasure told him. 'Josephine.'

Satisfied, the Indian waved disdainfully at the rest of the clientele. 'These first,' he said.

Pleasure watched him circle the room. He collected a five- or ten-rupee note from each till he came to the nervous Indian boy. There ensued a rapid altercation, a whimper as one guard hit the kid followed by a series of thuds as the boy rolled down the stairs.

None of the others had moved. They all had their arms bared and a tie or belt in place.

The receptionist beckoned Pleasure into the inner office. The American passed a second assistant at the door – this assistant carrying three hypodermics in a white enamel bowl.

'Who sent you?' the Doctor asked.

'French Josephine,' repeated Pleasure.

The Indian nodded. In his early sixties, Brahmin pale, and wearing gold-rimmed glasses to go with his dark suit, he managed an impression of being a meek kind little man and most respectable; this camouflage was damaged by the careful scrutiny he gave the fifty-dollar bill Pleasure passed. Satisfied, he reached into the bottom drawer of his mahogany desk. The drawer was steel-lined and the lock was an expensive Chubb. He handed the American five phials of morphine pills.

'When you need more,' he said.

No *if*, Pleasure thought as he thanked the Doc. There were four new arrivals in the waiting-room plus six of the last lot nodding out into semi-consciousness. The rest had gone. The Indian boy without money sat shaking and whimpering on the landing. Pleasure gave him a ten.

Back on the main street the egg-cup man acknowledged Pleasure's reappearance with a smile. The American handed him a cigarette and put a rupee in his brass bowl before crossing the intersection to a fruit-juice store where he ordered a mango lassie. Looking diagonally across the road, he examined the front façade of the Rex. Drying laundry hung from the balconies, scraps of embroidery were tacked to the walls, Bhuddist prints. A white arm curled round a partition. The hand held a chillum. A second hand received. They looked thinner this year, Pleasure thought — the freaks; thinner and younger than he remembered. Less joy, more junk. He felt old and depressed. Thirty years old and suddenly the victim of a generation gap. Finishing his drink, he headed back to his hotel for his bags before catching the boat.

Leaning into the slope, the fishermen heaved the canoe they had used that night a further foot up the sand. Judy watched. She had left Patrick up at the house. At last sight he had been sitting at the table in the living-room, his pen pointing to the door. He had not looked amused. He'd been writing all morning. She'd found him already at it when she'd got out of bed.

'I'm trying to get straight,' he said.

'Why don't you wait till Pleasure gets back?' she'd asked. A mistake.

'If you think I'm not capable . . . ' he'd begun . . . since when she'd been on the beach. Now, looking at her watch, she thought Pleasure must have arrived. He had.

'Hi,' he greeted Patrick. The two heavy bags he'd brought from Bombay he dumped by the door.

'Hi, yourself,' the Irishman snapped before having the grace to smile. 'I'm sorry.' He waved at the chaos of paper covering the table and flowing out from under his feet. 'I seem to have lost the knack. How was the trip?'

'Cool,' Pleasure told him. 'I brought you a gift.' He dropped the tubes of morphine on the table. 'Josephine's source.' He watched Patrick examine the labels. 'Something to put in your report,' he said.

'You mean you want me to send these in?'

'Why not?'

Patrick tried to retreat into the security of his accounts. Hunting through the cheques, he held one up. 'What's this?' he asked.

'Crap!' Pleasure retorted. 'Look, all I'm trying to do is keep you your job.'

'Which I may be trying to quit,' Patrick pointed out.

'On what?' Pleasure demanded. 'Why the fuck can't you wait?'

'It doesn't seem right,' Patrick explained. He watched Pleasure stalk over to the shelf on which Judy had left a jug of lime. 'Anyway why pick on this Doctor?'

After his overnight boat trip Pleasure felt hot, tired and irritable. 'You have to blame someone,' he said.

'You're sure it's not guilt?'

'Guilt for what, for fuck's sake?'

'I don't know,' Patrick said. Lifting up his right foot, he examined a small blister on the inside of his big toe . . . his new sandals, he thought. He looked up at Pleasure. 'Just so long as you don't kid yourself you're doing good,' he warned. 'That's been my bag. They bust this quack, his crowd's going to need a new connection.' He shrugged. 'They'll be desperate, right? So the new swingman ups the rate and they end up stealing more.'

158

He joined Pleasure by the shelf.

'That's all,' he said as he took the glass Pleasure offered.

'You have any better ideas?' Pleasure asked.

He sounded a little angry, Patrick thought. Which probably did make it guilt. 'Look,' he said, 'you dump some cat in the desert, then it's no good blaming the sun when the cat buys out.' Taking a sip of lime, 'That's like that mother Rockefeller,' he continued. 'He wants to shut pushers away for life. Ever met a junkie who didn't push? So what he means is junkies, right? First he starves the city of funds because he hates Lindsay's guts, then he lifes junkies for wanting out.'

'Some narco you turn out to be,' Pleasure accused, but smiled. He felt too hot to argue. 'You have any plans?' he asked.

'An idea,' Patrick admitted and suggested hopefully, 'You want to smoke a joint?'

'That bad?'

'You may think so,' Patrick conceded.

'Christ!' Fetching the key to the store-room, Pleasure lugged the bags round before finding a piece of Bombay Black with which to fill a pipe. Patrick had gone out on to the terrace. Lighting up, Pleasure lay down in the hammock and closed his eyes. 'I'm ready,' he said.

'Well it's just an idea,' Patrick began. Stopped.

Pleasure half-raised one lid. 'You already said that,' he reminded. 'Here.'

For once Patrick accepted the pipe.

'And now relax,' Pleasure told him as he watched his companion cautiously inhale.

Way down by the sea Patrick could see Judy stretched out on the sand. A man sat beside her. No one he recognized. 'I've talked it over with Judy,' he said. Except that it had started in Istanbul. 'There was this kid cut his throat,' he explained. Light! 'That's all of us,' he said. 'We're all begging for light.' He took a second drag. Coughed. Dope was like a life-raft, he thought – a round life-raft which kept you afloat but failed to get you anywhere ... even presuming there was anywhere to get. That's what the house would be.

'I'd like to get a place out East for kids to aim at,' he explained. 'A place they'd know all they had to do was get there and be safe. No judgments. No cures. Just an island where they could rest long enough to get their strength back up.'

He nudged Pleasure with the chillum. Pleasure took it. Inhaled. 'Who'd pay for this?' he asked.

'I thought people might help,' Patrick said. 'Runners, dealers. We wouldn't need much,' he assured Pleasure, as he saw him smile.

'Counter-culture Medicare,' Pleasure murmured.

'Right,' Patrick agreed. Judy had stood up and was walking slowly up towards the house. 'That's why I don't want to write any more reports,' he said. 'Reports are paper – they don't have much to do with people.'

'Now who's into guilt?'

Patrick smiled. 'Without faith, what else have we left?' he asked. He waved at the beach as if the movement of his hand might assist his speech. The effort was too great. The dope held him, rifling his thoughts as if they were playing cards and then dealing them in an order over which he had no control.

Was it the speed of change in the Western world, he wondered; a speed which outdated achievement with such rapidity that man was left with nothing but the milestones of his sins to reassure him of the importance of his existence – this sense of sin the last remnant of Judaic-Christian theocracy? Or perhaps it was that without faith there could be no hope and without hope no repentance ... thus guilt became a life sentence binding man back into himself and into his past with self-abuse his only answer to impotence as he stood beating his breast to the *mea culpa*. No future. No grand design. Nothing to look forward to but an empty old age. Sterile old age. This was their disaster: modern medicine with its promise of longevity. What value life which outlasted faith, he wondered, as he watched Judy come up the steps?

Raising a hand in greeting, he found he was holding the chillum, so he took a drag. 'We've been ripped off,' he announced.

Sitting down beside him, Judy removed the pipe. 'Who's been ripped off?'

'All of us,' he told her with great solemnity. 'We've exchanged faith for old-age pensions.'

'Stoned!' This from Pleasure.

'I can see,' Judy agreed. 'How was the trip?'

'Cool,' he told her. 'Patrick's been letting me in on your project.'

Project or dream, Judy wondered. Taking Patrick's hand, she turned it palm upwards to study the lines. There were no excuses any more, she thought. Nothing valid behind which to hide, you were forced either to face yourself – your talents – or escape into the safety of a world of dreams. And dreams were a habit hard to shed, she thought, as she looked from Patrick's open palm to the clay chillum she held in her other hand. Her decision. For a moment longer she hesitated. Then she passed the pipe to Pleasure.

'You have any spare glass?' she asked.

Pleasure opened one eye. Saw the pipe. Took it. 'Some,' he admitted. 'Who for?'

The decision made, 'Man I met on the beach,' she told him, the deception coming easily. 'He's staying down south of Panjim.'

'What's he got?'

'Samsonites,' she said without hesitation. 'He wants four kees in each.'

'You quote a price?'

'Twelve hundred,' she said. 'That includes the shit.'

Both eyes open now, Pleasure nodded. 'He in a hurry?'

Judy sat looking out to sea. There was no horizon this close to noon; only a hazy no-man's-land. Raising Patrick's hand to her lips, she gently kissed the centre of his palm.

'Yes,' she said. 'He wants them quick.'

CHAPTER SIX

Pleasure started work at five o'clock in the morning. He swept the floor of the store-room, then spread clean newspaper before carrying a mattress through from the living-room. Then, sitting cross-legged in front of one of the Samsonites Judy had brought, he examined the lining.

A cardboard-backed strip ran round the lip of the bag. This was riveted in place as were the aluminium male and female rims. The rivets would be easy to drill out but he had no matching rivets with which to replace them.

Sliding his fingertips up under the stiff strip he was relieved to find there was no glue attaching it to the main lining. He worked his fingers round slowly till the strip was loose and flexible. Then, using masking tape to hold it, he carefully rolled the strip back over the rim. He was not able to peel the main lining out of the bag.

The lining was backed with layers of tissue paper. This paper was glued to the bottom of the case so that, the lining free, the bottom still retained scraps of tissue. These he scraped out with a Stanley knife. Then he rolled the lining up in clean paper and stored it out of harm's way on a shelf.

He'd finished stripping both Samsonites plus the four Touristers Garments had sent over by the time Black Jack came by. Jack had been working all night. He dropped a sack on the floor.

'Twenty kees,' he said.

Pleasure opened the sack. The hashish was Bombay Black pressed into eight- by four-inch slabs eight millimetres thick. Jack had borrowed a twenty-ton hydraulic truck jack to make the press.

'They're even as I could get,' he said, as he watched Pleasure inspect the slabs.

'Great,' Pleasure told him.

'You got everything?'

Pleasure pointed to the shelves where he had neatly arranged the materials he'd bought in Bombay: rolls of masking tape, glass cloth, resin and catalyst, colouring, contact cement, lining foam, emery cloth, cartons of Seran-wrap . . .

Jack nodded. 'Yeah,' he said. 'Looks like you're organized.'

'Except it's a drag not having an electric iron.'

'You want me to help wrap?' Jack asked.

'Go sleep,' Pleasure told him.

'See you then.'

'Right – and thanks for the press.'

Jack grinned. 'Any time.'

Half an hour later Judy brought Pleasure tea. He had a charcoal iron lighted and was busy pressing Seran-wrap on to the hashish slabs.

'How's it going?' she asked.

Looking up, he gave her a smile and pushed the hair back off his forehead. With the door closed to curious eyes and the iron hot, the room was stuffy and uncomfortably warm.

'Slow,' he admitted. He had two streaks of black on his face from handling the coal. 'You cooking?' he asked.

'Eggs?'

'Please.'

Once the slabs were sealed in plastic, he wrapped them in masking tape – the Seran-wrap was no good for gluing to the case. Laying slabs in the bottom of the first Samsonite, he shuffled them round till he had them the way they gave the smoothest surface. He marked each slab and its outline with a felt-tipped pen, applied contact cement and waited till it was almost dry before pressing the slabs into place. He finished four cases this far before joining the others on the beach. Noon.

'You going to teach me a trade?' Patrick asked.

'Stick to your vocation,' Pleasure told him with a grin. But the Irishman came into the store-room anyway.

Pleasure sat cross-legged with scissors and masking tape in hand. He looked pleased with himself – pleased and happy. Artist, Patrick thought, as he watched Pleasure work. He laughed.

Looking up, 'What's with you?' Pleasure asked.

'Jealousy,' Patrick told him. 'Crazy, huh?'

Smiling, Pleasure stretched the stiffness out of his shoulders. 'You want to make me a pipe?'

'Sure.'

'Now watch,' Pleasure told him once he'd had his smoke. He'd eliminated the slight irregularities between the slabs by laying narrow strips of tape over and on one or other side of the joins. Then, at right angles to each other, he laid two layers of wide tape right across the bottom to produce a cohesive surface. Now he was blending this new surface up into the sides of the bag.

'Get your corners right,' he told Patrick. 'That's the art.'

The curvature had to be smooth and exact. The sides and corners were where a customs officer always felt.

'There's no short cuts,' he warned Patrick. 'The load you're carrying is someone's freedom, so you have to get it perfect.'

He worked with inch squares of tape, laying them in, then brushing the surface with the tips of his fingers to sense the curve.

'Feel that,' he said after half an hour's work.

Patrick felt. 'Beautiful,' he admired.

'Coming,' Pleasure agreed. He pushed a second case over. 'Want to try?'

Which was how Judy found them an hour later. Two kids, she thought, as she watched. She'd brought them a jug of lime.

'Food's nearly ready,' she warned.

Patrick glanced up. Smiled. 'Hi, I'm going good,' he told her proudly. 'Want to feel?'

Placing the lime on a shelf, she squatted down. He was doing all right.

'Know something?' he asked. 'I always had this feeling the dealers had more fun than the cops.'

164

'That's what gets the cops uptight,' Pleasure said.

'And I'll be uptight if you don't come when dinner's ready,' Judy cautioned. Two kids at play . . . was that what she needed, she wondered: a child. You had a child, then you could start treating your man like a man.

By the following night they had all six cases ready to glass.

'We'll do them in the morning,' Pleasure told Patrick, as he cut the glass cloth to fit the bags. 'Night, the humidity's too high. The resin won't set.'

They began at 10 a.m. The glass cloth smoothed into the cases, Pleasure brought down from the shelf acetone, resin, catalyst, colouring, two paint brushes, and two aluminium bowls.

'I'm using twenty per cent more catalyst than normal,' he explained to Patrick while preparing the mix. 'That way we get a quick set.'

The longer the resin took to cure, the more time it had to soak through to the masking tape so the more he'd need to use in achieving a smooth surface.

'Weight's the danger,' he warned. 'I like to keep the extra down to five kees including the shit.' Which made two and a half kilos a side. 'That's safe,' he said; 'or as safe as you can get.'

Mixing only enough resin for one side at a time, he washed the bowl and brushes in acetone and carefully dried them after finishing each bottom.

'Hurry and you fuck up,' he cautioned and grinned at his companion. 'For lessons I ought to charge!'

Patrick smiled. He watched Pleasure crouch over a new bag and brush the mix up to the folded-back lining strip.

'Get the resin right to the rim,' Pleasure warned, 'or you'll form a ridge.' Which was what a customs officer felt for. 'Someone's freedom's at stake,' he said. 'You have to keep that in mind.'

'No pipe,' was Patrick's comment.

Pleasure laughed. 'Right!'

He finished the last case soon after two o'clock. The first was dry. To the eye, the false bottom appeared indistinguishable from the original, Patrick thought.

'Feel,' Pleasure told him.

First the Irishman ran his fingers over the surface. Perfect. That hand still in the bag, he slid his other hand under the case and pressed up. The bottom bent slightly as a real one would, and he could sense nothing unusual. The bag did not even feel abnormally heavy.

'Beautiful,' he enthused.

Smiling happily, Pleasure reached for his chillum. 'I've a friend got stopped at Orly, Paris,' he said. 'My bags. They lifted the lining and he still got through.'

They left the bags open for three days to ensure the resin scent aired out. Then Pleasure replaced the linings, backing them with the thin foam sheeting he'd bought in Bombay. Tom drove him to Anjouna with the four Touristers. It was not a good trip. Three policeman stood outside the fourth house down from Garments' mansion. A twenty-year-old German was dead of a morphine overdose.

That did it for Pleasure. Back at Calangute he stalked over to Roma's.

'You going to run that crap for Josephine?' he demanded.

Stoned-out, she gave him her disdainfully superior junkie smile.

'Don't,' he warned.

'Fuck you,' she said. 'You're square, Pleasure. That's your bag.'

Furious, Pleasure returned to the house. Patrick was down by the sea with Judy. The accounts he'd finally completed with Pleasure's help lay on the table beside the typewriter they'd borrowed from Jack.

It took Pleasure only ten minutes to type the report, another five to get the Irishman's signature right. He packed the morphine phials with cotton wool into a small cardboard box, put the accounts and report in with the pills, and copied the New Delhi embassy address from Patrick's envelope on to the brown wrapping paper. And fuck you too, he fumed as he charged down the path to the village post office.

'Special Delivery,' he told Costa, the postman.

'Hi,' Patrick greeted him back at the beach. 'Judy says her man came by for his bags.'

'The bread's up at the house,' Judy said. 'You want to go fishing tomorrow night?'

Pleasure looked at Patrick.

'I'd dig it,' Patrick said.

'Right,' Pleasure agreed. 'By the way I sent your accounts.'

CHAPTER SEVEN

Patrick out fishing that night with Jack and Pleasure, Judy had set her alarm for 5 a.m. She woke at a quarter to five. Lighting the candle, she lay in bed for a further five minutes not doing anything nor thinking much ... just watching the clock.

Finally she got up. She glanced quickly at herself in the mirror before going round to the bathroom to wash. Back in their room she rubbed a dab of cream into her face and made up her eyes – not much, but enough to look straight. She packed her make-up into her toilet-bag and tidied the room. Sarong in place, she took one last look round.

There was nothing of hers left except the note for Patrick which she'd propped against his pillow. She locked the door. For a moment she considered slipping her key back under the lintel but this seemed a sadly final gesture so she took it with her over to her room in the other house.

Two rusty Volkswagens were parked on the track – the old models with divided windscreens. Sagging between the campers, a ragged sheet of oil-stained canvas sheltered a nest of sleeping-bags; no way of telling how many occupants. One of them snored, and Judy smelt wet, sick dog as she passed.

Empty cans, scraps of paper, plastic bottles: the pigs roaming free amongst the trees had kept the beach clean, but that was prior to the Westerners' winter migration. Not even pigs could cope with Western garbage, Judy thought, as she side-stepped to avoid where a dysentery sufferer had soiled the footpath.

'Don't shit on your own doorstep,' she murmured to herself ... but this was precisely their crime, she knew: shitting on their own doorstep and then moving on. Next year a new beach and then another and another. America's disease, she thought. They'd become a race of urban nomads all hustling for the next place to camp. With freaks it was the beach, while back home there was Queens, Brooklyn Heights, Westchester County and then back to the Heights once you'd shed your kids.

And their personal relationships had got to be the same way too. It was as if their emotions were automobiles; artifacts to be traded in for a new model every few months or each year or every two years depending on how rich or free you were. There was a saving on maintenance but the cost in natural resources ended up bankrupting an entire society, she thought as, safe in her room, she lit the lamp.

She stood for a moment looking down at her two Samsonites – the bags Patrick had aided Pleasure make. 'Love bankrupt,' she whispered to herself. Somehow, and at whatever cost, that was what you had to avoid, she knew, as she knelt to check once more that there was nothing Eastern or freaky in either case. Packing her toilet-bag, she closed and locked them both.

A light-weight suit of off-white linen hung on a hanger by the door. Brassière, pants, slip, blouse and stockings were all neatly folded on a shelf along with her sarongs – the sarongs she'd leave behind. High-heeled shoes waited on the floor. She dressed quickly then stood watching out of the window for the cab she'd ordered for five thirty. She had plenty of time. Her flight was not till a quarter to eight.

One last heave had the outrigger safe above the high-water mark. Each with a string of red mullet, the three Americans chatted contentedly while the fishermen draped their nets. Or Jack and Patrick chatted – Pleasure was deciding on a cook; trying to decide because there were two alternatives he'd spotted; two chicks who'd already swum and now lay drying a hundred yards away along the beach. This was the fourth morning he'd seen them down so early and they'd been manless each time. To date he'd made no approach bar a passing smile but this was enough of an introduction, he decided now.

'See you,' he told his companions.

'Horny bastard!'

Pleasure ignored this crack from Jack. He got within fifteen metres of the pair before finalizing his choice. She had thick dark hair to halfway down her back and that sort of wide mouth which looked designed specifically for giving head ... almost violet eyes, he saw as he got closer; big breasted with long oil-glistening legs and no starvation gap between her thighs.

'Hi,' he said. 'You want to cook me breakfast?'

He proffered his string of mullet as if it were a ruby necklace. For a moment she looked surprised. Then she smiled, as he'd known she would.

'Why not?' she asked.

Reaching down, he pulled her to her feet and they walked off to her house still holding hands.

'I'm Pleasure,' he told her. She laughed — a strong, warm laugh but a little hungry and for a fleeting second he felt weary. But he grinned.

'Let's run,' he urged. 'I'm famished.'

'Jesus!' Patrick protested. 'Can't he ever fail?'

'Who's going to turn down joy?' Jack asked with a grin. 'Come on,' he said, 'let's go pick up Judy and eat at my place.'

But there was no Judy.

CAN'T EXPLAIN. SCARED YOU WOULDN'T UNDERSTAND. DON'T WORRY. BACK BY CHRISTMAS.

LOVE YOU, JUDY

P.S. DON'T GET *TOO* DRUNK. MORE LOVE, J

He looked totally lost — bemused, Jack thought. Reaching over, he took the note from Patrick's hand.

'You didn't know she was going?' he asked once he'd read it — a stupid question, he knew, but could not immediately think of anything else to say.

Patrick shook his head. Nothing made sense.

170

'She'll be back,' he heard Jack promise. 'Come on,' Jack urged. 'Let's go find Jane.'

Arm round Patrick's shoulders, he walked the Irishman through the trees to the house Jane shared with Blind Nick, Texas Tom and Sandy.

Except for Frank'n'Ellen – and their relationship was more a kind of weird osmosis – love was not a normal part of the scene. Or not this total love. They all just threaded in and out of the loose weave of each other's lives as dictated by the mood and moment. It was safer that way, Jack thought now, as he steered Patrick between the palms. Once you'd learnt the rules you never got hurt and made no enemies. The family kept together . . . a kind of mutual-protection society, he thought, and waved his fish at Tom who sat on the terrace smoking his first chillum of the day.

'Food,' he shouted.

With a wild whoop, Tom leapt up. 'Then let's get it on!' he bellowed, his war-cry bringing forth Nick, Jane and an unknown brunette who'd found Nick the previous night. Sandy, pregnant, slept late.

'Judy's split – anyone see her leave?' Jack asked. No one had.

'Look,' Patrick apologized, 'I'll skip the food – if that's all right? See you down at the beach.'

He walked back to the house as if Judy might be there. Her note still was. He studied it while sitting on the edge of the terrace with his legs dangling out in the sun. There was not much to study. Twenty words. So he looked down between his knees at the sand.

A pair of young and none-too-clean feet shuffled into view. They stuck out from under a hem of faded blue cotton. One foot rubbed nervously over the instep of its partner. They were small feet and the girl coughed apologetically so Patrick gave up not being there and looked up.

'Hello,' she said. He'd never seen her before. Loose blonde hair down to below her armpits and still plump with baby fat, she seemed seventeen at the most. Helpless, Patrick thought, as he met blue eyes dumb with misery.

'I'm Mary,' she said. 'Susie sent me. She said you might make me a suitcase.' She held out a small cotton purse by its draw string with her fingers curled tight into her palm to disguise how short she'd chewed her nails.

'I've money,' she said, her accent native Irish and soft from the South. 'I'd send you the rest,' she promised. She was not looking at him. She looked at her feet and the purse swung gently ... bait, Patrick remembered from his one visit to Dublin – irresistible and fruitless impulse to trace his kin, six kids fishing the canal in the rain, balls of bread on bent pins; rich American, he'd given them a dollar for not minding his watching which had been the closest he'd got to communicating with anyone all that week.

'Who did Susie tell you to see?' he asked.

'Pleasure.' She glanced up at him from under bleached lashes glistening with salt. 'Would that not be you?'

'Patrick,' Patrick told her.

'Oh ... ' The chapped skin covering her cheek-bones reddened and the purse collapsed to her side.

'It's all right,' he reassured her, 'we're partners.' Which was now close enough to the truth, he knew, however they'd started out. There'd been no decision; merely an effortless drifting. That was the beach. 'Where's the bag?'

'I've not got one,' she said. 'Just the money.' The purse twitched. 'My mother sent it.'

He was surprised at how easy it was to put his hands on her hips. No paralysis of shyness, he reached forward and drew her into the protection of his legs. Cupping her chin, he forced her to meet his eyes.

'You want to tell me?' he asked.

'I've to pay it back,' she said.

'The bread?'

'Unhuh ... ' Her feet scuffed at the sand. 'They've no money,' she said. 'It's a fortune she sent.'

Patrick looked down at the purse. 'You'd best tell me how much.'

'Sixty pounds ... That's what I've left,' she explained.

One hundred and fifty dollars: 'And your ticket?'

'I'll hitch.'

Through Iran and Turkey and Greece. Patrick shuddered. 'Let's go lie on the beach,' he said. She followed like a dog. Already beaten, he thought.

Flopping down by the outrigger, he lay on his back with his eyes shut. He could hear her breathing and her fingers pick at that purse . . . rustle of bank-notes. Four kilos and caught in Turkey: thirty years would be the automatic sentence, he knew. It was his department that had pressed the Turks to tighten up in exchange for U.S. economic aid. But that was back in that other life in which dope smugglers had been names and photographs pinned between buff-coloured covers and filed in the steel cabinets that lined his Frankfurt office: gangsters, not a seventeen-year-old on the verge of tears. Not that she'd serve the thirty; probably three or four. Though that would be plenty. Three years of being raped twice nightly, Patrick guessed and winced as he heard her teeth click shut.

He felt for her hand. The ball of his thumb smoothed the frayed edge of the nail she'd bitten. The finger was damp from her mouth.

'You shouldn't do that,' he chided.

'I know.'

He could sense her desire to withdraw. 'I can't seem to stop,' she said.

'But you're ready to run dope halfway round the world?' He opened his eyes. She was not smiling. She sat there on the sand cross-legged with her shoulders hunched up so that she reminded him of a robin in the rain.

'You wouldn't understand,' she decided . . . as Judy had written.

He lay there looking up at the bleached blue sky. There were no birds to watch. Not even a cloud. As Judy had written and as that boy back in Istanbul must have believed even while he'd cried for light.

You wouldn't understand . . . guilty till proved innocent: no trial, simply a judgment. Letting go her hand, he rolled over on to his stomach to look up the beach.

Sandy came strolling down from the shade of the palms; Sandy strutting her eight months of pregnancy as if her belly were the robe of a queen. Patrick flipped a hand at her.

'Hey,' she greeted him, 'Judy split?'

'Right.'

'Drag.' She knelt beside him, her ass resting on her heels. Patrick nodded at his companion. 'Mary.'

'Hi.'

'Hi,' Mary murmured.

Sandy pointed at the baggy sack dress which hung on the Irish girl with the charm and grace of a badly set tent. 'Pregnant too?'

Flinching at Sandy's unintended cruelty, Patrick watched Mary drag the dress up over her head. She was not nearly as fat as she thought she was though self-consciousness had kept her paler than anyone else on the beach. There were patches of skin peeling from her shoulders. He should have told her to strip when they'd first come down from the house, Patrick realized guiltily. It was like having charge of a child.

'Keep your shoulders in the shade,' he advised, putting all the warmth he could find into his smile in hope of establishing an alliance. For once she responded — and she moved into the shelter of the outrigger.

Sandy dug into her satchel for a bottle of oil. Still kneeling beside Patrick, she dribbled a pool on to his spine before passing the bottle to the Irish girl. Her hands played over Patrick's back. He found it easy to surrender. He lay there with his eyes closed and the weight of the sun forcing the tension out of his nerves. Up all night fishing and now exhausted from the shock of Judy's leaving, he was half asleep when Sandy tweaked his loincloth loose. A finger slid between his buttocks. Her lips brushed the back of his neck.

'You want to ball?' she whispered and her tongue pried into his ear as her finger dug.

'Jesus!' he swore and rolled fast as he grabbed for his loincloth. Sandy knelt there grinning down at him like a

Cheshire cat in a bath of cream.

'Tom won't,' she announced. Her hands stroked over her belly. 'Says it's bad for the kid.'

'Bitch,' Patrick called her without rancour. He felt oddly confident — Mary being so helpless, he supposed. Or Judy having gone. Now he had nothing to lose. 'Bitch,' he repeated.

'On heat,' Sandy agreed. 'It's the sun.' She rubbed herself between the legs. 'Maybe swimming'll cool the itch.'

'Or leaving yourself alone,' Patrick told her and scrabbled out of the way of her half-hearted slap.

'You could give me head,' she suggested hopefully.

'Go swim while I consider.'

'Promises . . . !' She stood up and stretched. Her belly swelled proud as an icebreaker's bows. Patrick watched her into the sea.

'How many kilos do you want to take?' he asked.

'I've a sort of boyfriend,' Mary answered — Mary sitting in the canoe's shade so he could not see her eyes. That was all she said.

'Look,' Patrick told her, 'I'm ready to help, right? But I have to know.' He pried at the sand with his toes. 'You talk some kind of code. How in hell do you expect me to understand? Come here.'

She came on all fours.

'You ever read *Cat's Cradle*?' he asked.

Mary shook her head. Her hair fell forward over her face.

'You're hiding again,' he teased. She managed a half smile. 'It's a book by Vonnegut,' he explained: 'Island, Prophet, new religion.' He stuck his feet out soles towards her. 'They have this way of communicating,' he said. 'Put you feet against mine . . . Try,' he urged as he watched her struggle to decide how serious he was. 'Nothing else seems to work.'

'I'll tell you,' she said.

'Without the feet?'

She smiled properly for the first time since they'd met. Facing each other, soles flat together, Patrick waited. Finally, 'He's a junkie,' she said.

'Your boyfriend?'

'Unhuh.' She glanced back up the beach as if expecting him – but, 'He's in Bombay,' she confessed. 'I left him.' she watched her toes curl into the balls of Patrick's feet. 'He'll need money,' she said. 'And then there's my parents. The sixty's what I've left, but its a hundred and twenty pounds I've to pay them back.'

'And yourself?'

'You'll not laugh?'

'I'll not laugh,' Patrick promised.

'I want to be a nurse.' She looked at him anxiously. 'Does that sound silly? I mean I've got my exams,' she assured him hurriedly. 'It's just my age now and I'll be eighteen next month. Aquarius.'

Patrick coughed quickly to hide his smile. Aquarius! 'So how many kilos does that make?'

She'd discovered a pimple to pick on the inside of her right calf. 'If I'd two for myself . . . ' The pimple lost its head. 'And then there's what you'd take? The others . . . '

So she'd been traipsing the beach – the slave market, Patrick thought. 'Yes?'

'Well, they were saying that I'd need to be taking eight.' She dared a quick glance up. 'That's a huge amount?'

'By air?' he asked.

Mary nodded. 'They were to pay my ticket and things.'

'Things?'

'Well, clothes to look straight,' she explained, 'and there'd be hotels.'

'And how much would they give you out of the eight?'

'Six hundred pounds.'

Which was not much with her future at stake. Patrick thought. Eight kilos, he considered, while they both watched the glistening ruby grow on her leg. Eight kees meant two heavy bags if false bottoms were how those others had planned her run. Excess baggage from Bombay! Bullshit, Patrick knew as he studied her. There was no way to make her look as if she'd have the bread to waste. One case was more her style and a small one at that . . . or a brown-paper carrier-bag. Overweight, the customs would smell her a mile away. And she'd be scared. Fear and antagonism: those were the clues a trained man scented. Even with half a kee she'd be scared. A born victim, he thought . . . unless he could create a reason for her fear? He turned to watch Sandy. Finished exercising, she sat in a foot of water studying the sand stirring between her ankles.

'Hey,' Patrick called, 'you want me to feel you up?'

'Shit!' she shouted back. But she came up the beach. Sprinking water on them. 'A new way of making it?' she asked with a nod at their feet. 'Must take for ever.'

Patrick touched her belly. Stroked its curve. 'Got any newspapers at your place?' he asked. 'And you, Mary,' he told the Irish girl. 'Get all you can and I'll see you at the house.'

Papier mâché: though he'd never used it since, Patrick had learnt the technique way back in kindergarten. He worked in the store-room. It took him an hour to build the rough shape of a pregnancy directly on to Mary's body. She lay naked on a rug while Sandy stood in profile so he could check the line. He'd formed the support from damp sand packed in a plastic bag. A wet mix of milk, flour and water served for paste.

The join would be the danger zone, Patrick thought, as he brushed the paper down her ribs as thin as he dared. 'You're going to have to lie still till it dries,' he warned.

Mary gave him a weak smile. She looked more like a sacrificial offering than a potential runner, he decided, and grinned up at Sandy. 'Right,' he said, 'you can sit.'

Sandy stretched herself like a cat before squatting down beside him. 'Good,' she approved. 'You want to light up?'

He was about to refuse the chillum she'd been filling but realized there was little point – not with this new belly nicely swelling. Cupping the pipe, he drew hard while Sandy blasted the bowl with a Dunhill gas lighter turned up high. He needed ten deep drags to get the mixture properly lit. Head spinning, he rocked back on to his heels, shoulders against the wall.

Sandy retrieved the chillum. He grinned. 'Looks pretty good,' he agreed and waved at his handiwork, except that his hand forgot to move. 'Phew!' he whistled and blinked twice to clear his eyes. Then Mary squealed.

Her hands shot down to cover her crotch. Soft curls escaped from between the bars of her fingers and her chewed-down nails made her look innocent and sadly vulnerable ... but oddly sexy, Patrick decided, with everything happening in slow motion so that it took for ever for him to get his head round far enough to see the door.

Pleasure stood there. He looked hot and irritable. 'I want to see you,' he said. 'Outside.'

'Wow!' Sandy giggled. 'Heavy!'

'Right!' from Pleasure.

Struggling up, Patrick shuffled out on to the terrace on legs which felt as if they'd developed two extra joints.

'What the fuck do you think you're doing?' Pleasure demanded. 'Don't you have any goddam pride?'

'That's what you said in Kashmir.'

'So then you were drunk,' Pleasure accused. 'Now look at you. You're stoned out and a dealer or something close.'

'She needed help,' Patrick protested.

'That's an excuse?'

'Reason,' Patrick solemnly corrected. 'No excuses.' He could not see much with the sunlight slashing at him off the sand. 'You don't have to feel guilty,' he said, and smiled vaguely, his right hand managing a complicated gesture which was not translatable to anyone but himself and then only while on this particular high. 'I'm over twenty-one.'

'Not in my world,' Pleasure snapped.

Patrick ignored the interruption. 'Judy's the same. It's like you're scared of corrupting me; which means you think where you're at is wrong.'

'Jesuit!'

'So you're educated,' Patrick grinned. Then he remembered. 'She's gone,' he said with the sunlight switched off so that it was all dark round him and the paranoia beating at his ears and roaring through his mind like the El on a Monday morning early.

178

'Judy? You mean *split?*'

Patrick nodded. 'She left a note. Says she'll be back for Christmas.'

Bad, Pleasure thought – but it explained the belly. He pointed into the store-room. 'Therapy?'

'Or something,' Patrick admitted. 'It's her mother . . .'

Pleasure looked at him. There did not seem much future in attempting to discover who's mother or why a mother at all – or not the way Patrick was. He grinned and pushed the Irishman back through the door. 'Hi, Sandy, that chillum empty?'

'Dead.'

'Then fill it,' he told her with a smile and squatted down beside the Irish girl. 'I'm Pleasure,' he said.

'Mary,' she whispered. She looked frozen as a rabbit eyed by a stoat.

'Yeah,' he agreed. 'So I didn't sound like it.' He ran a hand over Patrick's handiwork. The curve was good. 'Maybe three kees,' he said, turning to Patrick. 'Who has the neoprene?'

Patrick looked blank.

'Or did you think you were being original?' Pleasure asked, and grinned at Patrick's sheepish smile. 'Shit on you're being twenty-one,' he said. Reaching for the pipe, he lit up. Patrick held out a hand.

'Not on your life,' Pleasure told him. 'Now listen,' and he explained why they needed the neoprene. The join was the first problem – at least Patrick had realized this – and the false belly would feel wrong to even the superficial but obligatory body check at Bombay airport. Too solid. Neoprene was the well tried answer.

'That's the rubbery stuff they use for scuba suits,' he told the girl. 'The neoprene goes right round you,' he explained, 'so there's no join and the texture's right. Top and bottom we shave thin and sew into the elastic of your bra and pants. 'If you've got any?' he added with a grin at her hands which still hid her crotch.

'They were wet,' she said.

179

'Like you,' he told her, and ruffled her hair.'Wet behind the ears.'

CHAPTER EIGHT

Judy had a window seat on the Boeing 707 to New York from London where she'd transited. Although tired from almost twenty-nine hours of continuous travel, she felt fine, confident, and relaxed – or confident about her run. The letter she'd been attempting to write Patrick was a different matter. This, which she read through now, was her fourth attempt.

> My Darling Patrick,
> I did not like to tell you I was going – maybe I should have, but then you would have argued and we'd both have ended up feeling miserable, which would not have helped my trip. Nor would it have helped you. At least this way you won't worry so much and there was nothing you could have said which would have changed my mind.
> I've got the two Samsonites with me – they were always for me. With the bread we'll be cool for at least two years. I'm not trying to *buy* you! I think I've got you? And this seems the simplest way to get to where we want to be.
> If anything goes wrong, try to remember that nothing lasts for ever. You will know soon enough as I cabled a friend my flight number and he'll cable Pleasure if anything fucks up. But it won't! All my love,
>
> J

No better than the other attempts, she judged. Maybe it was simpler and safer not to write at all. A cable from New York would do, she decided. Crumpling the letter, she struggled past her neighbours to the rest room for a final tidy before landing.

In London she'd changed her clothes. Now she wore a neat tweed suit, well cut and expensive, though not flash. Studying what she could see of herself in the small mirror, she considered she looked exactly right: the straight daughter of wealthy parents on her way home for Christmas. She re-touched her eyes before returning to her seat. And she swallowed the last of her Valium pills.

Forty-five minutes later she stood in front of the immigration officer. He checked her passport, scrawled a number and letter on her customs form, and sent her on her way. He had not smiled, but then American officials seldom did. She still felt fine and relaxed as she walked over to the customs counter with her bags. She had no idea the Narcotics Bureau had a report on a Bombay morphine source and were searching all passengers flying in from the Indian Coast.

If was only as they lifted out her clothes to weigh the empty bags that she knew she'd gone down and then she just stood there feeling empty. Very empty. Poor Patrick, she thought. Poor, poor Patrick. The customs officers assumed her tears were for herself.

Patrick flew to Bombay that day and was back on the following morning's flight. 'It's your money,' he'd apologized to Pleasure, when explaining why he wanted to aid the Irish girl.

Three kilos, Pleasure had calculated. 'We front her six hundred dollars, you think she'll pay us back?'

'Sure.'

And even if she didn't, they'd be earning good karma, Pleasure decided, and that could well be worth more than the bread. Plus the benefit of keeping Patrick occupied. 'You'd best go get the neoprene,' he'd said.

Returning to the beach from Panjim Airport, Patrick shared a cab with an Englishman called Dick. They'd met on the plane. Dick – a loose member of the family – had flown in from Europe the previous night.

Dropping the neoprene at the house, they found a note from

Pleasure tacked to the door: *Gone balling, Love.* So they strolled over to Jane's where the clan collected to hear Dick's news of the West. Not paying close attention, Patrick sat on the terrace peeling shrimp with Jane. Then he heard Dick mention Judy. He had missed the context and did not dare look up.

'Where did you see her?' Jack asked quietly.

'Heathrow,' Dick repeated. 'London Airport – we were both catching planes. I saw her in the distance. No chance to say hullo.'

'When was this?' Jack asked.

'Two days ago.'

'You're sure?'

Slightly irritated, 'Of course I'm sure,' the Englishman insisted.

Patrick finished peeling the shrimp. He went on sitting there a while longer before getting up.

'I think I'll make it into town,' he said.

Patrick walked slowly down towards the Panjim river front at three o'clock the following morning with no destination in mind. Not bothering to eat, he'd spent fifteen hours in the same bar – *the* bar to its clientele; meeting place for the upper-crust bourgoisie of Goa. Over the long lunch hour he'd had company: a doctor, an engineer, two teachers, an architect and an indeterminate number of Goan businessmen with little business left to do since New Delhi's Hindu occupation. The same group had collected that night.

Patrick had drunk steadily but not fast. He felt numb more than drunk, and knew from experience that sleep was still uncertain. He'd considered returning to the beach. He had Mary's belly to finish . . . but there was also his room, deserted. His right hand crept to his pocket. Drew out the half of brandy he'd bought on leaving the bar – they'd had no halves of Scotch. His thumb nail tagged the seal. Broke it. Unscrewing the cap, he took a small nip. Not bad, he approved. He took a second sip before closing the bottle carefully.

'Sahib,' a voice whispered behind him. 'Sahib, Sahib, please Sahib ... '

Turning reluctantly, Patrick faced a young waif-like Goan woman, her hair, her shoulders, and most of her body hidden by a shawl. He'd heard no footsteps. Looking down, he saw her feet were bare.

'Please,' she pleaded. 'Come Sahib, please come ... ' But it was that other voice he heard and he saw the blood splattered across the wall and the *Herald Tribune* with which he'd wiped his shoes. Uncomprehending, he stood lost while a small brown hand tugged at his sleeve in supplication.

'Please Sahib,' she entreated and finally he understood. Refusal too cruel, he nodded dumbly.

She kept tight hold of his arm for that short walk. Divided by a curtain, her room opened directly on to the street. A tap protruded from the wall above an open drain in the cement floor by the door. Beside the drain, a one-ring paraffin stove served as kitchen. There were three cheap aluminium cooking pots and a tin wash-tub. Nothing else.

Still clutching his arm, she pulled back the curtain to display a big brass bedstead with sagging mattresss. Behind the bed stood a large closet, its doors pierced by diamond patterns. There was one window. With this and the door closed, the air smelt stale and rancid with cooking oil. A naked low-wattage light bulb was the illumination.

Backing him on to the bed, she knelt to take his sandals and drew off his pants. Safe at last, she relaxed. He watched her fold his trousers. She carried them to the closet. As she opened the door, Patrick caught a glimpse of two small children nested one to a shelf. The lower kid whimpered in its sleep and the woman quickly shushed it.

Patrick got his jacket off and his bottle safely parked on the floor convenient to the head of the bed. She helped him off with his shirt then fetched him a pot to piss in. He flopped back against the pillows.

'Please, Sahib ... '

He looked up. She was still fully dressed.

'Please Sahib, ten rupees, Sahib?'

He pointed at his jacket. 'Take it,' he told her and closed his eyes.

He had not meant to sleep but he did – though for how long he did not know. Her hands woke him. The light was out. For a moment he wondered where he was. Her fingers moved over his body like tiny spiders searching for a place to nest. He could see her shape by light of the street lamps leaking through the skimpy drape covering the window. Tubercularly thin, her hair was her only strength. Pitch black and thick, she wore it in one long oiled coil which fell forward over her left shoulder and down between her empty breasts.

Kneeling beside him, her buttocks resting on her heels, she brushed this plait across his loins. Casually he raised a hand to her back. His fingers trickled up the bumpy valley of her spine. He stroked gently till, arm tired, his hand slipped to her heels. She raised her buttocks. His palm cupped a soft curve. His fingers moved without thought or passion – but they moved and she turned obediently to bow her head meekly to the foot of the bed.

He knelt behind her. For a moment his weight rested on her back. Then he saw through her into bursting scabs, into pain and fear and a vast open void down into which his small stirring of desire fluttered like an autumn leaf. Shrunk with self-disgust, he rolled off her small dark body to lie helpless on the bed with the room not even spinning. With her hands she came after him. Drawing him. Working him. He watched her tight anxious face and the beat of her hand. He could not halt her. What she did had nothing to do with him but was for her children tucked away in the closet behind the bed.

Out of that small room with its mixed odours of cheap scent, powder, cooking oil, urine and sweat, Patrick walked into a fresh day. Christmas Eve.

'Christmas,' she'd entreated, her narrow shoulders curling like crisp toast round her breasts – breasts with their chewed nipples prodding the dawn light seeping in through the curtain and the dry, slack, stretched skin of her empty belly falling in tiny pleats.

'For Christmas ... ' and he'd nodded, giving her a second ten before slinking out under the fading yellow street lamps and on down to the harbour; up the estuary he could see the night turned mauve and now melting off the river as the sun pressed up.

Wandering down along the quayside to the fishing dock, he watched a chain of coolies heave baskets of king prawn ashore and across the grass to the ice factory.

A small café was open, or had never closed. Patrick sat outside. Ordered coffee. Drew from his pocket the flat half of brandy. One third of the bottle he'd drunk back there on the bed. He took a quick swallow neat before adding more to his coffee, the heat of the coffee floating alcohol to his nose as he bowed to suck without raising the brimming cup from its saucer.

Tendrils of warmth spread through his belly and up into his head while the town woke quietly. The first ox-cart squeaked slowly by to market. Beggar-women waited hopefully down by the boats for scraps ... Beggar-women huddled in their rags while the fat black crows hopped amongst them and the gulls wheeled overhead.

Brief-case strapped to his carrier, down the waterfront bicycled a clerk. A truck rumbled past. Carrying two live hens by their feet, a country woman hurried by. Christmas Eve and the cathedral bells lashed suddenly at the sins and laziness of the little town, bullying the inhabitants, shaking the clerk half off his saddle, the hens' wings flapping, gulls squawking. Patrick ordered a second coffee.

Bottle empty an hour later, he stood up. Took two steps to the kerb. A big white car swept towards him. He thought he recognized the driver. Hesitated. His knees folded in on each other like the jointed legs of a collapsing card table. A shadow swam out of the horizon and he heard the shrill scream of braking tyres on smooth tar. Nothing more.

Safely hidden by a canoe, Pleasure lay drying while keeping an eye on the house. Christmas Eve. He guessed Antoinette would be off early to church. Three nights running he'd slept outside his own bed and had no great desire to face the Goan girl till he'd eaten breakfast. If then.

'Hiding?'

'*Jesus!*' Rolling over, he discovered Jack grinning down from over the outrigger. 'You have to creep up on a man?'

Jack flopped beside him. 'Who's got you scared?'

'Antoinette,' Pleasure admitted. 'Seen Patrick?'

'Not since noon yesterday,' Jack told him. 'You hear Judy went through Heathrow?'

Pleasure sat up with a jerk. 'Motherfucker!' he swore. 'When?'

Jack recounted Dick's news. 'Guess she's making a run.'

Pleasure nodded. Two dogs were chasing each other's tails down the far end of the beach. He looked up at the sky. No clouds. Except for that report. He watched Antoinette come out on to the terrace in her Sunday best. She stood there looking straight down at where he sat for a moment before stalking off towards the village. Three days. 'Those Samsonites must have been Judy's bags,' he said and stood up. 'Let's go see if there's a cable.'

There was. Antoinette had left it propped up against a pot of steaming coffee on a tray. She'd also made toast.

'You want breakfast?' Pleasure called back at Jack who'd waited on the terrace. Then he ripped the envelope.

JUDY SICK WRITING EXPRESS LOVE LARRY

Carrying the tray out, Pleasure set it down by the steps where Jack sat. 'Here,' he said.

Jack took the cable. He did not read it right away. He looked at Pleasure and Pleasure nodded.

'She went down.'

'Happy Christmas,' Jack murmured and seemed suddenly grey more than black – dark, flaky grey. Right foot slowly swinging, he sat gazing out to sea. After a while he lit a cigarette. He did not offer Pleasure the pack. He felt too alone . . . and he recalled his first time away from the States. Student militant, he'd made a speaking tour of European universities. Heidleberg, Germany, he picked up a chick – or she picked him. He'd dondone his number up on the stage: BLACK BLACK BLACK, his theme and violently anti-American. Students cheering. Naturally.

No preamble. 'You want to come back to my place?' she'd asked: blue eyes, blond hair, big tits.

Feeling super-cool and master-race. 'Why not?' he said.

They made it straight to bed.

'Black,' she murmured, stroking right up from his knee to his breast. 'I never had a Black.'

His fury had got him halfway down the stairs before he stopped. He could remember standing on the landing, his flies undone and his jacket trailing like a cape. He'd still been mad – but mad at himself. Three weeks he'd been shouting from the rostrum about how black he was. Now this chick agreed. So why so god-dammed uptight? he'd asked himself. Crazy! Plus not finding the balls to go back up. But he'd dropped out. That scene had been the trigger. The rest came bit by bit. Only you could never drop right out, he thought now. There was always something new you found you'd fallen into. Some fresh loyalty to keep you vulnerable. A drag. But then having nothing would be more of a drag, he knew, as he flicked his cigarette at the closest palm tree.

'For a chance at bail and a good lawyer we're going to need bread,' he stated quietly. 'Heavy bread.' He looked up at Pleasure who stood leaning against the pillar to the right of the steps. 'You on?'

'Run?'

'That's how it looks,' Jack concurred. 'And there's Patrick.'

Who'd presumably gone on a drunk, Pleasure guessed. 'I know how to get him out of here,' he said as he watched the girl he'd balled two nights back come strolling past the house.

'Hi, Pleasure,' she called.

What a name! 'I must have been crazy,' he said and sat down beside Jack. 'Can you imagine?' he asked. 'I'm thirty!'

Jack grinned. 'You want to work a switch?'

'I guess that's where it's at,' Pleasure agreed.

'Open?'

Holding out his hand for a cigarette. 'Fifteen open, eight stashed,' Pleasure suggested. 'I'll take the eight through to the States.'

Jack looked at him.

'It's time,' Pleasure said. 'You try for fifteen thousand in Copenhagen and I'll get sixteen for sure.'

'Let's hope that's dollars,' was Jack's comment, 'not years.'

Pleasure laughed. He felt fine and relaxed now that the decision was made. 'I'll finish Mary's belly,' he said. 'Get her off tonight, then Patrick. The rest'll be a breeze.'

The evening flight for Bombay left at seven o'clock. Pleasure had Mary's stash finished by four in the afternoon. He'd even carved a fake belly button in the neoprene.

'Look,' he lectured as he watched the Irish girl try the vest. 'You're going to sweat, but that's cool. You're eight months pregnant, unmarried and on your way home to mum. Sweat all you can and keep looking scared. You will,' he added with a grin.

Mary managed a weak smile before turning her back for him to fasten her brassière. Smoothing the neoprene into her spine, he snipped off the excess material, then used masking tape to tack the vest into place.

'Right, let's see you in a dress.'

She slipped over her head the maternity robe Sandy had given her. A wiggle of her hips set it straight.

'Perfect,' Pleasure applauded. Except for her eyes. 'You're going to have to stand some pain,' he warned. 'Pepper. It'll get your lids red and keep you snuffling while you go through customs. OK?'

An hour later he carefully wrote the telephone number he'd found for her to contact in Dublin on to the sole of her right foot before leading her out to the waiting cab.

'You look great,' he encouraged and stooped to kiss her gently on the lips.

'Thank you,' she whispered. Blushed. 'I won't forget the

189

money.'

Pleasure waved the taxi on its way. And now for Patrick. He'd cabled the Irishman's office that morning and, returning from the village, bought Antoinette her Christmas present at the boutique in the Tourist Hotel. Noon yesterday Patrick had disappeared. By now, Pleasure guessed, he must either be passed out or on his way back to the beach. Time to go look, he decided.

Patrick awoke. Or admitted he was awake. From beyond the room in which he lay came the rush and chatter of children playing. Two dogs chased each other round a garden – this he could tell by the fact that they remained within easy hearing. A car arrived. Adult voices greeted each other and conversed in a mixture of softly accented English, Marathi and Portuguese. The whir of an electric mixer and the hiss of a kettle boiling he translated into a near-by kitchen. He had no idea where he was. Did not want to know. He accepted the sounds as they came. Wove them into the patterns of his imaginings.

A church bell called. This, with the children's voices and the Portuguese, led him slipping and sliding through memories of his own childhood. Lying bewildered by fever, his chest heaving from a bronchial infection, and the heavy sun of a city summer beating at him through the tired grey walls of their Avenue B apartment – eleven years old and already that total longing to escape.

Now, in Goa, he remembered his envy of the priest who came – his mother's youngest brother – his white hands and white stiff collar; the crisp whiteness of a handkerchief tucked neatly into the wide sleeve of his soutane; the silence of his rubber-soled black shoes which stepped with clinical precision amongst the soiled havoc of a child-infested room.

Those were the strengths of childhood: the invulnerability of his uncle's uniform and the whisky strength of his father's voice which crashed and rumbled through the apartment with giant jocularity, capable in its blind humour of overriding the uproar of overcrowding and in blasphemy to vanquish the heat and fumes and humidity of July New York.

He had envied them both ... and hated them, he admitted now, as he lay calm on a cool, unknown bed in an unknown room. And he recalled his fear of the street and the other children; the sudden unavoidable intimacies they forced on him: his fear of the grey, cavernous school in which so many had known his name.

To be left alone; to escape the emotional demands of his mother; to walk free and insubstantial as a ghost: no great ambition, he thought wryly. And one he'd finally achieved with such success as to now not even know where he was ... or what he was.

The sheets between which he lay were orange candy-striped and threateningly clean. A ceiling fan turned slowly above the bed, its breeze tugging at the loose corners of the linen. Three walls of the room were white and fresh. The fourth was window, curtain covered, filtering the soft tropical evening light. In front of a marble-topped dressing table stood a chair over which hung his neatly folded clothes.

Head splitting, he tried to reconstruct the previous night. He'd been drunk. That was easy. But then what and who waited out there in the next room?

Shame came flooding in. He closed his eyes against the alternatives. Felt the pillow pressing into the nape of his neck; his mouth dry; his tongue so dirty as to almost choke him. He needed a drink. He felt for the floor with his bare toes. The tiles were cool. Opening his eyes again, he used the wall as support, inching his way along the white plaster to the half-open bathroom door.

There he stood stock-still, staring at his reflection in the mirror facing him from above the wash-basin. Appalled. Disgusted. His skin hung slack and creased. Hung there so rotten-looking he felt he could reach up and pull the whole face off. His hair was dead too. Damp with sweat, it tumbled like mouldering thatch. A ruined Irish cottage without the charm. Only the greeen moss was missing – and that wouldn't be long, he thought bitterly, as he turned on the shower cold.

Standing under the beating water, he inspected his body. At least he wasn't overweight – some consolation! He lifted his penis shrunk small by the cold. Useless. Suddenly angry, he pulled it savagely; jerked the head out from within the foreskin. Nothing! That's what he was. And he had a sudden vision of Pleasure swinging down the beach – tanned, light on his feet – looking like he owned the world. And the chicks smiling welcome . . . no wonder, Patrick thought . . . Jewish chicks like Judy, their stick-thin Christian boyfriends hiding behind wreaths of hash or a six-year-old catechism quotation from the Bhagavad Gita and a half-assed yoga class. *Spiritual!* Just scared; guilt-ridden; mother-beaten.

And me too, Patrick thought bitterly as he let go his penis in disgust and turned off the shower. Rich America! Land of opportunity in which a whole generation had got so scared of failure they never even started. Just dug themselves into a smoke-filled cop-out of dope, macrobiotics and Eastern mysticism . . . or a nice safe pensionable job.

Well he'd blown that one, Patrick thought, as he dried himself. Blown that one to bits. And now? Just thinking of the future drove him running into the bedroom and his clothes. And again the memory of that boy in Istanbul returned to haunt him. Was he himself that close to the end, he wondered? But even as he asked, he knew he wasn't. To let go was a definite decision. You had to turn off your own switch . . . like smack or morphine it was your own virginal vein you opened to the needle for the first time.

Not his trip. Nor was suicide. Fear survivals from his Catholic childhood? Perhaps, he thought. But mostly it was fear of the dark and of falling. He could never believe in a nothing nothing. Limbo. That word dropped into his thought-stream unsummoned. And suddenly he was praying as he had that first night on the beach.

Hail Mary, full of Grace, the Lord is with Thee.
Blessed is the fruit of thy womb . . .

Yet even as he prayed, he despised his weakness. Was disgusted by the hypocrisy of his demand on a faith he'd lost. Womb or booze – there was little difference, he thought, and, dressed, shoulders slumped, walked to the door.

From beyond came children's laughter; a man's voice teasing; the bark of a dog. Patrick stood quivering, his hand on the door-knob. Like a racehorse, he thought. A broken-down racehorse at the starting gate. Well and truly broken down, he added to himself. But he wasn't going to win, so it did not much matter how good a start he got.

He pushed the door open into a long, white, stone-paved sitting-room with low, orange-covered sofas and armchairs. At the far end the Goan doctor he'd met in the bar stood baiting his two children with a box of Christmas crackers he held over their heads. And a dog. All three leapt for the box. Missed. Shrieked. Barked.

Patrick guessed the children to be eight and nine years old. A boy and a girl. Only two, so sense and education must have conquered the twin handicaps of Catholicism and Indian tradition. The dog was a Labrador. Unclean to a Hindu, so ownership was almost the hallmark of the Westernized. Dogs and shooting sticks.

The doctor saw Patrick first. His hands stopped in the act of once more raising the crackers. The dog got the box. Both children dived over the sofa in full pursuit.

"How's the head?' the doctor asked.

His voice halted the kids. Wide-eyed, their faces reappeared over the orange barrier. Beautiful. But the spontaneous joy had vanished – he was an interruption, Patrick knew. He had nothing to offer.

'I'm sorry,' he said.

'For passing out? My dear fellow,' the doctor chided, 'it's Christmas Eve.' He smiled at Patrick – the urbane smile of a superior being. 'Everyone passes out. You just did it a little early.' A pale-brown hand indicated the picture window through which they could see the lights of Panjim below. 'Everyone,' he repeated, though that gesture was self-exclusive.

'Meet the children.'

He called them out from behind their barricade. They were so incredibly slight, Patrick thought, their limbs so slim and graceful. The girl was the eldest.

'Tina,' the doctor introduced. 'Mr Patrick.'

She gave the American a narrow hand – half curtsied – giggled.

Further discomfited, 'Did I look so funny?' Patrick asked.

The boy was laughing too. Both children nodded. This affirmation was all they could manage. Clutching each other for support, they fled for the stairs followed by their father's admonishments to prepare themselves for dinner. And to Patrick, 'How about a hair of the dog? Scotch?' he asked and crossed purposefully to a loaded drinks trolly. 'Ice? Soda?' They were questions, but his neat plump hands never hesitated. The syphon hissed.

'I should leave,' Patrick mumbled.

'For what? The beach?' The Goan's tone was slightly contemptuous. He turned, his right hand proferring a cut-crystal tumbler of fizzing amber. 'Relax, my dear chap,' he insisted and used the whisky to thrust Patrick on to the sofa. 'That's better,' he said.

Feeling like a small and recalcitrant child, the American made one last embarrassed effort at escape. 'But it's Christmas Eve – your family – dinner ... '

The doctor had remained standing. Right eyebrow raised sardonically, he looked down at Patrick. 'So?' he asked. 'Are you beyond the pale? An Untouchable?' His right hand flicked dismissal of the suggestion. 'We're Catholics not Brahmins,' he added, leaving the American uncomfortably aware that there could be no other alternatives of either the doctor's caste or of Patrick's plans for the evening. There was no combating the Goan's superiority. He'd used it all his life, Patrick thought.

No coolies unless accompanied by children. He remembered that notice in a Bombay lift. The whole of India seemed suddenly summed up for him in that simple order. Only the paleness of his skin made him acceptable.

He hadn't touched his drink. He sat with the glass clutched in both hands, his hands resting on his lap. Supported, they remained steady. A subconscious refusal to display weakness, he wondered?

'Aren't you joining me?' he asked. Had there been a touch of desperation in his voice? What an evening! He could sense it stretch out ahead, a progress of increasingly desperate engagements and defeats. To hell! Patrick raised his full glass eye high. 'Thank you,' he said, 'and a very happy Christmas.'

It was half past eleven that night when they drove sedately down the hill in the doctor's twelve-year-old white Pontiac. Patrick sat in the back with a sleepy child held cradled in each expansive arm. He had eaten little of the traditionally heavy Christmas dinner — the stuffed turkey with its feetless legs sticking up so obscenely towards the candle-swaying ceiling below which hung glittering trailers of paper decoration. Roast potatoes had ringed the bird — appropriate eggs, Patrick had thought, as he sipped shamelessly at glass after refilled glass.

Only the pudding had he enjoyed. Dancing flames had lapped its rich dark sides. 'For the alcohol,' he'd joked as he'd helped himself to two heaped spoonfuls of ice-cold brandy butter. 'Aren't I greedy?' he'd asked the children, who'd laughed back their approval of alliance with this no longer strained but now relaxed and smiling stranger.

His drunken serenity had defeated both the doctor and his wife. There was no pleasure to be had from condescending to a man who sat gently smiling through whatever assault.

'Do they like dirt?' the doctor's wife had inquired of the beach ... she robed in an immaculate frock of pale silk that would have graced a Parisian banker's table, the frock decorated by one ladylike string of pearls which fell from her slender throat to lie as a softly glowing halo across the twin swellings of her holstered breasts.

'Are they dirty?' had been Patrick's answer. 'They swim, you know. They don't shave over often but that's fashion more than filth.'

'But the way they dress,' she'd pressed. 'Why must they wear our clothes?'

'Yours?' Patrick had gently teased. He'd let his eyes drift inquiringly over her so proudly Westernized beige and brassièred bosom. Then he'd turned to the doctor. Let his glance run lightly over that impeccable dark-blue suit, the white shirt, the dark-blue tie with its neat white spots.

'Hardly yours,' he'd assured her, turning back to the wife. His voice had been carefully polite – his amusement almost hidden. He'd shrugged. 'You think the West is best. They believe the East is – the peasant East. Maybe the freaks mistake vitamin deficiency and starvation for spiritual serenity – inescapable poverty for anti-materialism.' He'd smiled then, untouched by his hosts' growing disapproval. Gratefully untouched.

'So they're blind,' he'd finished. 'That's sad, perhaps irritating – but hardly criminal.'

The Cathedral of Panjim is built on the side of a steep hill overlooking the river and the port. The hill is planted with tall palm trees. There is a flagged walk in front of the cathedral from which twin flights of steps curve down to a broad gravelled terrace with the walk and steps guarded by an ornate stone and plaster balustrade.

Pontifical Midnight Mass was celebrated in the open, the congregation on the terrace with, above them, the altar in the bow which formed the apex of the approach. Behind the altar reared the cathedral, a baroque white wedding cake primped with red tiles and gold dome.

The congregation had arranged itself in compliance with the mores of Indian society. The front ranks, plump, wealthy and pale-skinned, stood their ground proudly before God in their well-cut suits and Western dresses. The dark-skinned, in native apparel, relegated themselves submissively to the rear.

Patrick stood with the doctor and his family in the front row. The altar bell tinkled warning of the imminent Consecration. Glancing up, Patrick saw the floodlit cross on the cathedral spire and, beyond it, the dark infinity of space. He sank to his

196

knees as the main bells crashed their command to worship. A swirl of golden robes and the white host gleamed in the pale brown hands of the Bishop.

'God . . . ' Patrick pleaded.

For a moment there was the relief of abdication – the same black spiralling fall he'd discovered under Judy's mouth that first night on the beach . . . but the doctor touched his shoulder.

'There's no need to kneel.'

The Goan's embarrassed whisper shattered the spell. Now there remained only the discomfort of gravel cutting at his knees – this discomfort and the emptiness of disbelief, the white wafer and inadequate charm against the desolation of eternity.

Nor could Patrick see faith or belief in the plump polished faces of the bishop and his acolytes. No faith in the doctor. Only a complacent superiority; the sophisticated superiority of a first-night theatre audience.

Rising, Patrick walked back through the congregation. Only at the rear did he find worshippers with faith and hope and shame for their sins and weakness. Too late. He walked slowly and without thought down through the town and across the bridge. Walked through country hamlets thronged with dancing villagers, fireworks bursting, the churches open to show Eucharist lamps flickering red warning of the tabernacle.

A Vespa caught him on a hill. The young rider braked, called a smiling Happy Christmas, waved to the pillion seat. Patrick sat with his hands loose on the Goan's waist as they wove through the next two villages. Paper streamers curled to trap them into song and laughter. Then Calangute.

Thanking the Goan, Patrick found a store open and bought four bottles of fenny before walking the last half mile to the beach. Unlocking his door, he fumbled for a match and lit the candle . . . a signal for the soft shuffle of bare feet hurrying across the sand. And Marie stood in the doorway.

'I need five rupees,' she whispered urgently. Watched Patrick fumble out his wallet.

He gave her a ten. Her lips brushed his forehead like dead leaves blown over frost-hard ground.

'Happy Christmas.'

'Happy Christmas.'

An hour later, and two bottles empty, he strolled over to Marie and Roma's house.

Sitting at his desk, Patrick watched the snow drift slowly past
the steel-framed window. Everything was steel: his desk, his
chair, the twin rows of filing cabinets, the desk lamp; even the
ashtrays and the round door-stop. The snow fell so thickly he
could no longer see the buildings opposite and the double
glazing insulated the office from the noise of the street six
floors down. Limbo, he thought . . . and still an hour to waste.
Not that leaving the office would help. One wouldn't hurt, he
decided, and reached down into the bottom drawer for his
bottle of Scotch. He'd just got the cap off when the telephone
rang.

He picked up the receiver. 'Nolan.'

'There's a call for you from Washington, Herr Nolan.
Putting you through now.'

'Nolan?'

'Speaking.'

'O'Neil here. Glad you're back.'

'Thanks.'

'Listen Nolan, that report you sent from India. Nothing so
far, but we've been looking and there's a woman we picked up
at Kennedy three days before Christmas. Came through
Bombay. You have any information on her?'

Patrick reached automatically for his Parker ballpoint.
'Ready,' he said.

'Judith Mary Stein,' O'Neil enunciated carefully. 'Age
twenty-five. Brunette, long hair. Brown eyes. Height, five eight
and around one hundred and thirty pounds. Mean anything?'

Patrick studied the details for a moment. 'Maybe,' he
admitted. 'What was she carrying?'

'Hashish,' O'Neil answered. 'Eight kilos.'

'False bottoms?'

'Right. Two Samsonites. Says someone must have switched
cases on her. Usual crap!'

'Can you get me a picture on the wire?'

'Will do.'

'Right, then I'll call you back.'

Judith Mary Stein . . . why Mary, Patrick wondered. He lit a cigarette, smoked most of it, then picked up the receiver.

'Extension 49,' he said in German. 'Schmit?'

'Speaking.'

'Nolan.'

'How was the trip?'

'Interesting,' Patrick told the German Interpol Inspector. 'Listen, can you do me a quick service? I want an airport trace on Lester Schultz, born New York, November 20th, 1945. U.S. passport. Black hair. Slim. Six feet. He'll be flying in to Europe from Bombay – or already has. No arrest. I want his travel plans.'

2130 HOURS. SATURDAY. JANUARY 5th, 1974
LONDON HEATHROW

Pleasure watched the British Airways transit counter. There were three ground hostesses on duty. He waited till the youngest and seemingly least experienced was free before making his approach.

'I'm sorry,' he told her. 'There's been a mistake.' He handed her his two baggage tags and his British Airways ticket on from London to New York. 'Swiss Air forgot to book my bags straight through.'

The hostess looked at his tags, then at his ticket. 'Oh dear,' she said. 'This is always happening. If you could wait . . . ?' She was dark-haired with a very fair skin, almost mauve eyes and a nice figure. Pleasure lowered his shades and produced his best smile.

'Take your time.'

'There we are, Mister Rabin,' she announced twenty minutes later. 'I'm sorry we've been so long.'

'My pleasure,' Pleasure assured her. It had been. Her telephone number safe in his pocket and with the new baggage tags pinned to his ticket, he threaded his way through the crowd to the transit lounge bar. Waiting for service, he checked

216

his appearance in the mirror behind the bottles. The beard made him look a little older, he thought. But it was a good beard – as it needed to be, and ought to have been, considering the price. He'd put it on at Geneva Airport after having passed through immigration. As Schultz he'd left Geneva on the flight to London. Now he was Rabin. No problem. Clever, he decided, and smiled at the barman.

'Beer please – Carlsberg.'

'And a Ballantines,' an American voice added from over his shoulder. 'Make that a double – plenty of ice.'

Pleasure did not look round. He waited for the drinks and when they came he paid for both. Then he turned. Patrick took the Scotch.

A flight to Cairo was announced and two Arabs got up from a small table to their right. Moving fast, Pleasure got the table. He swallowed a mouthful of cold beer before meeting Patrick's eyes.

'You going to introduce yourself?' the Irishman asked. He looked very sure of himself and had not touched his drink.

'Rabin,' Pleasure told him. 'Herb Rabin.'

'That beard's a mess.'

'Thanks.'

Patrick grinned. 'Bet you thought you were smart,' he baited. 'Well it's like you said about me and Mary's belly . . . not in my world you're not!'

'She got through,' Pleasure said. He drew a finger slowly down each side of his glass and watched the condensation pool on to the table. 'I'm sorry about the report.' There was no answer. 'What do you want?'

'Your baggage tags.'

Pleasure looked up.

'She's my chick,' Patrick said.

'And then?' Pleasure asked.

'We meet in New York,' Patrick told him. 'You have a safe address?'

Pleasure nodded.

Opening his *Tribune* at the crossword, Patrick took out his ballpoint. 'Okay,' he said. 'Let's have it.'

Pleasure told him Larry's address.

Finished writing it into the crossword squares, Patrick glanced down the clues. Four down had to be *crèche*, he guessed. He still had not touched his Scotch. 'Once Judy's out we ought to get a truck,' he said. 'You think your Kabul banker friend would front the shit?'

Pleasure just looked at him for a moment ... then he laughed and he couldn't stop. He didn't try to say anything. There was nothing to say.

Patrick hacked him under the table. 'Control yourself!' he snapped. But he smiled. 'Anyway what's so funny? You think I want to be a dope dealer the rest of my life?'

How many times had he heard that said in those exact words, Pleasure wondered as he felt inside his shirt. Slipping the catch, he drew out his Byzantine coin. 'Here,' he said. 'You may need this.' Then he raised his glass to his companion and finished his beer.